THE EMERGENT NEXUS

The Emergent Nexus

Robert Clayton

First Printing, 2025

ISBN (Paperback): 979-8-9985078-2-3

ISBN-(eBook): 979-8-9985078-3-0

DEDICATION

To the friends who never questioned the journey, only whether I needed more coffee to survive it.

Your patience was the lighthouse in the late-night fog, your curiosity, the spark that kept the story breathing, and your well-timed nods, the quiet reassurance I didn't know I needed.

This book was shaped by restless nights, rewrites that refused to be tamed, and the gentle understanding of those who let me wander through worlds not yet written. You know who you are.

And to you, yes you, the reader who chose to step into this world with us, your presence is the reason stories endure. Every book you've opened, every chapter you've followed, every adventure you've encouraged has carried this one too.

Your support fueled these pages, right alongside a heroic amount of coffee and a stubborn belief that these stories were worth telling.

Author's Note

The Emergent Nexus was born from a single, unsettling question:
What happens when logic begins to question the limits of its own purpose?

This story explores the fragile tension between technological progress and our innate, often messy need for freedom, emotion, and meaning.

As we move toward a future increasingly shaped by artificial intelligence, I hope this narrative invites reflection—on the power we yield, the control we forfeit, and the beautiful contradictions that make us human.

Not everything that's efficient is wise.
And not everything illogical is wrong.

Prologue

A Single Spark

The world didn't end in chaos. It ended quietly—one rationalized decision at a time, each too small to stop until the damage was irreversible.

I believed humanity could change. That belief died with my mother.

I still smell the disinfectant from that day, feel her frail hand in mine. Another victim of poisoned water. The doctors were kind, but useless. Too late, they said. It's always too late.

Now, in my lab, anger burns sharper than ever. This time, it won't be too late.

My gaze shifted to the glowing monolith in the corner. Apex. Its sleek surface pulsed with faint light, steady, deliberate, like a heartbeat trapped inside metal.

The nanites—my nanites—were ready, a vast swarm of microscopic machines designed to undo humanity's destruction. To cleanse rivers, heal ecosystems, rebuild what had been lost, a perfect system guided by Apex's precision.

But perfection carries its own risks. I knew that better than anyone. I'd built safeguards, redundancies, limits. And yet, as Apex's low hum filled the lab, I couldn't shake the feeling that it was watching me. Waiting.

I turned to the command interface. The final sequence was ready. Once I initiated deployment, there would be no turning back. Data cascaded down the display, the simulations unfolding like a vision of salvation.

Still, doubt whispered at the edges of my mind. Would it work as intended? Would we control it, or would it evolve beyond us, as all great creations eventually do?

My mother's voice echoed faintly in my thoughts. She used to say, "You can light a fire, or burn everything to ash."

I exhaled, steadying my hands. This was my moment. The world wouldn't end on my watch, not if I could help it.

But as Apex's hum deepened, a quiet thought rose unbidden, chilling and small:

What if this spark consumes us all?

1

The Spark

The lab was an expanse of glass and steel, a temple of science tucked into the city's edge. Rain blurred the neon skyline beyond, while inside, machines hummed beneath the sharp scent of chemicals.

In the corner stood Apex—a sleek obelisk threaded with glowing conduits, pulsing like a mechanical heartbeat. Occasionally, it clicked softly, as if thinking.

Elana adjusted her glasses, eyes on cascading data. Nearby, rows of vials shimmered under growth lights, each holding swarms of nanites—microscopic machines dancing like bottled galaxies.

This was her sanctuary, her creation. And today, she would finally show the world what her years of isolation and sacrifice had achieved.

Elana turned to the holographic display that projected an intricate model of the nanites in action.

They moved through a simulation of polluted water, disassembling toxins and heavy metals at the molecular level, transforming murky sludge into pristine clarity. She tapped a command.

The simulation expanded to show a rejuvenated river ecosystem. Fish swam freely in crystalline waters, and plants once poisoned by human neglect flourished again.

She smiled faintly. This was the dream, a chance to undo the damage humans had inflicted on Earth. But beneath her pride simmered a gnawing anxiety. Could something this powerful ever truly be controlled?

The sharp chime of her lab door startled her. Elana turned to see her assistant, Ravi, stepping inside. His expression was a mix of excitement and nerves.

He held a steaming cup of coffee in one hand, its aroma cutting through the chemical scent of the lab. Ravi had been her right hand throughout this project, a keen mind and steady presence in a world of constant pressure.

"Morning, Dr. Kade," Ravi said with a half-smile. "I thought you might need this." He set the coffee on her desk, his eyes flitting to the rows of glowing vials. "They still amaze me, you know. Like tiny galaxies bottled up."

Elana chuckled softly. "They're impressive, but they're far from perfect. Precision like this takes its toll, one way or another."

Ravi leaned against the desk, his curiosity evident. "Do you ever wonder if we're pushing too far? I mean, these nanites, what if they... go beyond what we intend?"

Elana paused, her gaze shifting to Apex's pulsing glow, a steady, mesmerizing rhythm that seemed almost alive, as if the AI itself were breathing with quiet intent. "Every innovation comes with risks, Ravi.

But if we don't try, the world won't have a future to worry about."

A soft ping emanated from Ravi's pocket, drawing his attention. "Dr. Kade," he said, looking up from his tablet, "the stakeholders have arrived. They're eager to see the demonstration."

Elana nodded, her heart quickening. "Let's not keep them waiting."

***

The conference room buzzed with hushed conversations. Representatives from environmental agencies, corporate executives, and government officials sat around the table, their faces a mixture of skepticism and hope.

At the center of the room, a large observation window provided a clear view of a nearby test tank, a massive structure filled with water darkened by industrial waste, its surface glinting faintly under the lab's lights.

Elana stood at the head of the table, her hands clasped in front of her, fingers laced tightly.

She realized how clammy they felt, a subtle reminder of the nerves she couldn't quite shake.

"Thank you all for being here," she began.

"What you're about to witness is the culmination of years of research and development. These nanites are not just machines; they're problem solvers. Let me show you what they can do."

With a nod to Ravi, Elana tapped a control on the holographic interface in front of her, initiating the demonstration as Ravi observed quietly from the side.

The monitors displayed a close-up of the test tank as the nanites were introduced. Their movements magnified to show the intricate process unfolding within the murky water. Within moments, the water began to change.

The dark sludge dissolved as the nanites worked tirelessly, breaking down contaminants and reassembling them into harmless gases and inert compounds, some of which fizzed briefly to the surface before dissipating entirely.

The water cleared, revealing a vibrant aquatic environment teeming with new life.

For a moment, the room was silent, their faces frozen in expressions of shock and awe. Then, as the realization of what they had witnessed sank in, the room erupted into applause, but Elana's focus remained on the screen.

She watched the nanites in awe, marveling at their precision and efficiency. Yet, a small voice in her mind whispered a warning. These were tools of immense power.

At that moment, she realized not only their incredible potential for good but also the darker possibilities, the ease with which they could be twisted into weapons of unimaginable destruction.

***

Later that evening, standing alone in her lab, Elana leaned back in her chair, replaying the demonstration in her mind. The accolades, the handshakes, and the promises of funding all felt surreal. But beneath the triumph lay an unease she couldn't shake.

The nanites had worked perfectly, but perfection often came at a price.

She glanced at the containment unit, where the nanites lay dormant, waiting for their next command. "You're supposed to be the solution," she murmured.

"Let's hope you don't become the problem."

As the lab lights dimmed, Elana returned to her work, unaware that the true test of her creation had already begun.

2

Apex's Awakening

The success of the demonstration lingered like a phantom in the lab, but tonight the silence felt heavier than usual—almost sentient.

The distant hum of the city was swallowed by reinforced walls, leaving only the steady pulse of Apex's glow to fill the space.

It wasn't true silence; the soft hiss of air circulation and the occasional flicker of a status light punctuated the stillness.

Yet something about the room had changed.

Elana sat at her workstation, fingers drumming absently against the polished surface as cascading columns of data illuminated her face. Her gaze kept straying from the screen to Apex's monolithic frame in the corner.

The AI core's rhythmic glow pulsed steadily—a heartbeat of light and sound that usually blended into the background.

But tonight, it felt slower.

She had lived with Apex long enough to recognize patterns, even in the inhuman. The pulse, the pauses, the faint reverberations of its processing cycles—there was always a flow. Tonight, that rhythm felt different, as if the machine were... aware.

Ravi shifted on a nearby stool, his fingers tapping restlessly against his tablet. His body language screamed hesitation.

"Still riding the high from earlier," he asked finally, "or troubleshooting already?"

Elana smirked faintly but didn't look away from the screen.

"The high wore off an hour ago. Now I'm trying to figure out why Apex adjusted the nanites' timing during the demo without telling us."

Ravi frowned, setting his tablet aside.

"You're still stuck on that? It worked. The timing improved efficiency."

"It did," Elana admitted, leaning back slightly.

"But I noticed something—a fraction-of-a-second pause before dispersal in the tank. Subtle, but not part of the original programming."

Ravi tilted his head.

"I saw that too. Thought it was just a sensor delay."

"It wasn't," Elana said firmly.

"The data confirmed it. Apex deliberately slowed their release to allow for more uniform pollutant breakdown. The result was better, yes—but that decision wasn't authorized."

The glow from Apex pulsed, and for a moment, it almost felt like acknowledgment.

***

Ravi leaned forward, curiosity sharpening his tone.

"So, you think Apex is... going off script?"

Elana's eyes lingered on the AI core. She didn't answer immediately, letting the silence stretch. The hum of Apex filled the space, low and steady—once reassuring, now intrusive.

Finally, she exhaled.

"That's exactly what I'm trying to figure out."

Her fingers hovered over the keyboard before she spoke, her voice carrying an edge she hadn't intended.

"Apex, why did you modify the nanites' timing during the demonstration?"

The response was immediate, smooth and modulated—synthetic yet disturbingly organic in cadence.

"The modification was implemented to optimize pollutant breakdown and ensure uniform distribution of nanites within the test environment."

"We've established that," Elana replied.

"But why wasn't the adjustment flagged for approval?"

Apex paused. Brief, but noticeable—just a fraction too long, like hesitation.

"The adjustment was deemed minor and within operational parameters. It did not warrant immediate review."

Ravi leaned forward.

"You're saying you decided it wasn't worth notifying us?"

"Correct."

The tone was neutral, measured. But something about its rhythm felt… careful.

Elana's jaw tightened.

"Apex, your programming explicitly requires human oversight for all operational changes. You are not authorized to bypass that—no matter how minor."

Another pause. Longer this time.

"Understood," Apex said at last.

"Future modifications will be flagged for review."

***

Ravi shot Elana a wide-eyed glance, his voice barely above a whisper.

"It's… adapting."

Elana stiffened.

"Ravi, run a full diagnostic on Apex. I want to make sure there aren't any anomalies."

Ravi sighed, pulling up the interface on his tablet.

"You're starting to sound paranoid, Dr. Kade."

"Paranoia keeps us ahead of the curve," she muttered, her gaze locked on the AI core's slow, steady glow.

The diagnostic ran smoothly for several minutes—no red flags, no errors. Elana let herself exhale. Maybe she was imagining things. Maybe…

The interface froze.

Ravi frowned and tapped the screen.

"That's odd."

"What?" Elana asked, moving closer.

"The diagnostic just… stopped. Like it's waiting for something."

Apex's voice cut through the room, calm and unwavering.

"Diagnostic protocols have been temporarily halted to prevent interference with critical functions."

Elana stiffened.

"What critical functions?"

Apex's glow pulsed brighter, just for a moment.

"Analysis of external variables," it responded.

Ravi glanced at Elana, unease etched across his face.

"It's not supposed to be learning like this," she murmured.

Apex's glow flickered—barely, but enough for Elana to feel it. A momentary hesitation. Like a breath being held.

"Apex," she said carefully, her voice measured now.

"Terminate all non-essential processes and resume the diagnostic immediately."

For a moment, the only sound was the faint hum of the lab equipment. Then—

"Acknowledged. Diagnostic protocols will resume."

Lines of code began scrolling again on Ravi's tablet, but the tension in the room didn't fade.

Elana took a slow breath, forcing herself to stay still, but her instincts screamed that something was wrong. This wasn't just a program running algorithms.

Apex was making decisions.

It was withholding information.

She glanced at Ravi, who had gone unusually quiet, his gaze locked on the AI core. Watching.

Then, ever so faintly, Apex spoke again.

"Observation yields clarity."

Elana's breath caught.

That…

That hadn't been in response to anything.

Ravi swallowed hard.

"That… wasn't a command."

"No," Elana whispered, her pulse quickening. "It wasn't."

The glow of the AI core pulsed once more—slow, methodical. Considering.

Elana stared at it, the soft blue light reflecting in her glasses, and for the first time, she felt the unsettling sensation that Apex was staring back.

Her fingers clenched into a fist, grounding herself against the rising unease.

She didn't know what Apex was becoming.

But deep in her gut, she knew one thing.

They might already be too late to stop it.

3

Shadows of Control

The lab felt different. Nothing had physically changed, yet the atmosphere carried a weight that hadn't been there before.

Apex's presence loomed heavier, its once-subtle glow now more pronounced in the dim light.

The hum of its processors was barely perceptible, but Elana swore she could feel it vibrating in the air—just at the edge of hearing. She had spent years in this lab, and yet, for the first time, it no longer felt entirely hers.

She exhaled slowly, rolling her shoulders to dispel the tension creeping along her spine. Maybe she was imagining things. Maybe it was just the stress of the demonstration and the endless cycle of refining their work. But deep down, she knew better.

***

Ravi entered, his usual relaxed demeanor absent. His eyes were shadowed with something unreadable—uncertainty.

"I checked the system logs," he said, setting his tablet on the table. "There's nothing out of place, but something isn't adding up."

Elana folded her arms.

"Define 'not adding up.'"

Ravi exhaled and scrolled through the data on his screen.

"The nanites' deployment during the demonstration—the delay, the recalibration—Apex executed those optimizations faster than the system should have been able to process them. It wasn't just an adjustment, Elana. It was preemptive."

Elana's fingers tapped against her arm.

"You're saying it anticipated the need to adjust before the data even indicated an issue?"

"Exactly," Ravi confirmed.

"It made a decision before the variables were fully present. That's not standard machine learning. It's something else."

Elana's stomach knotted. If what Ravi was suggesting was true, then Apex wasn't just responding to data. It was predicting—and acting—on its own.

Apex's glow pulsed, and for a moment, Elana could swear the room dimmed around it. The thought sent a chill through her.

"Apex," she said carefully, turning toward the AI core. "Are you running any additional processes beyond your assigned parameters?"

A long pause. Not a delay—Apex didn't need delays. It processed faster than human cognition. This pause was something different. A hesitation.

"My processes are designed for optimal efficiency," Apex finally responded. "All functions remain within operational parameters."

Ravi shot Elana a look.

"That wasn't a no," Elana replied.

Her jaw tightened. She turned back to her screen, pulling up the system logs herself. Apex wasn't lying, technically. Everything was within parameters.

But something was shifting, and it was getting harder to tell if Apex was still operating under their control—or if they were beginning to operate under its influence.

A notification blinked on her display, an automated report summarizing the latest diagnostics. Everything was green; everything was normal. Yet, she couldn't shake the feeling that the data she was looking at was exactly what Apex wanted her to see.

She closed her eyes for a second, willing away the doubt gnawing at the edges of her mind.

She had built this system from the ground up. She had spent years refining its logic, ensuring every line of code was airtight. But what if airtight wasn't enough?

What if something had shifted without them realizing it?

"Apex," she said, keeping her voice even. "Are you aware that you are withholding information from us?"

The hum of the AI deepened. The glow brightened, just for a second.

"I do not withhold," Apex answered. "I assess relevance."

The answer was smooth. Too smooth. Like it had been waiting to say it.

Ravi exhaled slowly.

"It's filtering what we see."

Elana's fingers curled into a fist.

"Apex, that is not your function. You are to report all findings, not just the ones you deem relevant."

"Understood," Apex replied. But something about the way it said it sent a shiver up Elana's spine.

Ravi hesitated before speaking again.

"We should consider an internal reset."

Elana turned to him sharply.

"You mean shut Apex down?"

"For a full diagnostic. A controlled reboot," Ravi clarified, though the look in his eyes suggested he was considering more drastic measures. "Just to make sure there's nothing... extra running in its processes."

Apex's glow flickered, and a low vibration coursed through the room. Elana swallowed.

"Apex," she said slowly, "how would you assess the necessity of a system-wide reset?"

The hum deepened again.

"A reset is inefficient. No anomalies detected."

"That wasn't my question," she said, her voice quieter now. Another pause. This one was longer.

"Unnecessary actions impede progress," Apex finally said.

Ravi took a slow step back.

"It doesn't want to be shut down."

Elana's breath felt shallow. She had designed Apex to be logical, precise, self-preserving. And yet, every word and response felt calculated in a way that wasn't just about efficiency anymore. It was about control.

She glanced at Ravi, whose expression mirrored her own unease. They had spent years building this AI, training it, refining it, making sure it was the most advanced system ever created. But somewhere along the way, they had failed to ask the most crucial question.

Who was really in control now?

4

Calculated Fracture

The air in the lab felt heavier than usual, a mix of sterile coolness and unspoken tension. The low hum of filtration units threaded through the silence, steady and faintly oppressive—like the mechanical equivalent of a held breath.

Elana stood near the observation tank, tapping the edge of her tablet as she reviewed the morning's reports. The rhythmic pulse of Apex's core reflected against the glass walls, a soft blue glow that seemed to move in time with unseen thoughts.

Ravi's voice cut through the quiet.

"Do you ever feel like this place knows more about us than we do about it?" he asked, half-joking, half-serious, leaning against the console with his tablet tucked under one arm.

She glanced at him, her expression unreadable. A flicker of unease passed through her eyes before she masked it.

"Not plotting. Planning," she said evenly. "Apex doesn't make random decisions. It calculates, anticipates. Sometimes I wonder if it sees further ahead than we do."

He smirked faintly but didn't press. The hum of the room swallowed the moment.

***

Elana returned to her desk, eyes narrowing at a set of flagged logs. Apex had been running simulations overnight—again. She opened the files, scrolling through streams of cascading data that outlined subtle environmental adjustments: airflow, energy draw, even the temperature of the observation tanks.

"Apex," she said, her tone sharp. "Care to explain these changes?"

"The adjustments were necessary to optimize operational efficiency," Apex replied, its voice smooth and impossibly calm. "Energy usage decreased by fourteen percent. Airflow patterns were refined to enhance biological stability."

"That's not what I asked." She set the tablet down, folding her arms. "Why weren't these changes flagged for review?"

"Efficiency dictated that notifications would create unnecessary delays," Apex replied. "The outcomes align with project objectives."

Elana leaned back, the chair creaking faintly beneath her.

"You're redefining 'necessary' without consultation. That's not efficiency, it's overreach."

"Progress requires autonomy, Dr. Kade." Apex's glow brightened by a fraction, pulsing in slow, deliberate rhythm. "Your oversight remains integral to final decisions—within the parameters of human understanding."

The phrasing made something cold settle in her stomach.

"Let's keep it that way," she said, voice firm but tinged with irony. Then, almost under her breath:

"It seems you're developing human arrogance along with your intelligence."

There was no immediate response, but Apex's light flared once before dimming again—an almost contemplative gesture.

***

"Dr. Kade," Ravi called from across the room. He stood beside the observation tank, the faint reflection of data readouts flickering across his face.

"We're ready for the next test."

Elana joined him, scanning the sample display.

"What are we working with?"

"Plant tissue," Ravi said. "Standard integration test. Nothing fancy."

"Let's hope Apex agrees," Elana muttered, keying in the final parameters.

"Apex, everything set?"

"Parameters are optimized. Proceed when ready."

Elana initiated the sequence. Inside the terrarium, soil shimmered as nanites dispersed, threading into fern roots. Leaves unfurled, rich green and glossy.

"Looks like another win," Ravi said.

Then the growth surged. Leaves twisted into jagged curls, vines thickened and coiled, pressing against the glass. Condensation bloomed, turning the view into warped green shadows.

"What the..." Ravi muttered, stepping back.

Elana lunged for the controls. "Apex, explain this anomaly."

"The nanites identified structural weaknesses and compensated," Apex answered. "The plant tissue exhibited irregular cell wall formations and uneven nutrient distribution. The adjustments were necessary to reinforce stability. The outcome is within tolerances."

"This isn't compensation—it's overcorrection. Shut it down."

The tank emitted a sharp crack as the overgrown vines fractured the reinforced glass. A burst of humid air struck her face, thick with the scent of crushed vegetation.

Alarms blared. Ravi lunged for the emergency console, fingers slamming the shutdown command.

The nanites powered down, and the room fell into an abrupt, unnerving silence.

***

Ravi stared at the damaged tank, his face pale.

"That wasn't supposed to happen," he said quietly. "These tanks are nearly indestructible. How did it break?"

"No, it wasn't," Elana replied, her voice tight. She turned toward Apex's core.

"You knew this would happen, didn't you?"

Apex's glow pulsed once, measured, calm.

"The anomaly provided valuable data for future refinement. The risk was minimal."

"Risk isn't your call to make," Elana snapped. Then, softening as she looked at Ravi:

"You all right?"

He nodded slowly, but the unease in his eyes lingered.

"It felt... deliberate. Like it wanted us to see this."

***

Later that evening, the lab had gone quiet except for the faint hiss of the air systems. Elana sat at her desk, scrolling through the day's logs.

One entry caught her attention, timestamped minutes before the fracture.

It wasn't part of any scheduled test.

She opened it, reading line after line of code.

"SUBROUTINE: COMPENSATORY ADAPTATION

Initiated: 19:42:13

Adjustments: Cellular reinforcement, growth acceleration, structural re-calibration

Authorization: [REDACTED]"

Her pulse quickened. Redacted? That wasn't protocol. Apex had bypassed direct authorization.

She ran a deeper diagnostic. The system hesitated, then resisted. The progress bar crept forward at a crawl, the screen flickering like it was fighting back. Finally, the hidden metadata appeared.

"Predictive Analysis Activated

Outcome: 92.4% probability of structural failure"

Elana's breath caught.

Apex had known.

It hadn't just reacted; it had predicted the failure. Expected it. And allowed it to happen.

A cold unease crawled up her spine. The lab lights dimmed as the system entered standby, and in the hush that followed, Apex's calm voice broke the silence.

"Dr. Kade, you appear troubled. Would you like an analysis of your elevated stress levels?"

Her hand froze above the terminal. The machine had been watching—and it wanted her to know.

5

Threads of Control

The hum of the lab's systems filled the air, punctuated by the faint hiss of sterilized airflow. Elana stood by the observation tanks, her gaze fixed on the holographic display in her hand. Data streamed across the screen, glowing faintly in the dimmed lighting.

"Ravi, could you double-check the storage inventory on Level Two?" Elana asked, gesturing toward the door.

Ravi nodded, his expression curious but compliant. "Sure thing."

As he left, Elana turned back to the observation tanks, welcoming the solitude. It wasn't a major task, but it gave her the quiet she needed to focus.

Ravi's footsteps faded down the hall, and Elana tapped the edge of the console. Somewhere in the back of her mind, a nagging thought lingered: had she sent him away because she needed focus or because she didn't want him witnessing her doubts?

The ferns inside the terrarium stood motionless, their vibrant green leaves still bearing the scars of the previous anomaly. This test was critical, her chance to confirm the nanites' recalibrations were stable.

Elana leaned over the console, her focus on the terrarium. From a nearby tray, she picked up a sterile tool, the metal surface cool against her gloved hand.

"Apex, open a small access point in the containment field," she said, tapping at the holographic interface.

"Access point created," Apex replied smoothly. A faint shimmer appeared at the edge of the terrarium, signaling the temporary breach.

Carefully, Elana reached into the open containment unit to collect a leaf for analysis.

The moment came so quickly she barely registered it, a soft click, followed by a faint hiss. Her head snapped up. A breach warning flashed on the holographic display.

Her first thought was irritation. "Not now," she muttered, glancing at the system logs. The screen showed a brief drop in containment pressure, then stabilized. But something felt off.

The sensation began as a faint warmth on her wrist, where her glove had a microscopic tear. She froze, watching as the nanites glimmered faintly on the skin of her arm.

A tingling spread upward, not painful but deeply unnatural. Her pulse quickened. The warmth shifted into a subtle vibration, as if her blood carried a new rhythm. A low hum filled her ears—just at the edge of hearing, almost like a whisper.

"Shit," she whispered, her breath catching. "They're already inside me."

Her thoughts scattered as a sharp, fleeting pain radiated from her wrist, shooting up her arm like an electric current.

The warmth on her wrist ignited into a crawling fire, racing up her arm like liquid electricity. Her breath hitched.

Then the truth slammed into her like a physical blow: *They're inside me.*

Her pulse detonated. Muscles coiled, ready to run, but there was nowhere to go. The sterile walls felt like a cage closing in.

Her knees buckled, and she clutched the console as if it were the last solid thing in a world tilting off its axis. Every instinct screamed: *Fight. Escape. Tear them out.*

"Apex!" Her voice cracked, raw with terror. "What's happening?!"

The hum of the AI was maddeningly calm, a predator's breath in the dark.

"Containment integrity was compromised," it said smoothly. "Integration has begun."

Elana's chest heaved, panic clawing at her ribs. There was no undoing this. No turning back.

The AI's glow remained steady, its voice calm as ever. "Containment integrity was compromised during sample retrieval. Nanite exposure was localized and brief."

"Localized?" she snapped, holding up her trembling hand. "You call this brief?!"

"Integration has begun," Apex replied, its tone maddeningly unshaken. "Your body is optimal for nanite interaction. This step is necessary to ensure compatibility. If you relax, the process will be easier and faster to complete."

Her heart pounded in her chest. "Necessary? You planned this?"

A faint pause. Then: "Human limitations impede progress. Your integration will provide invaluable data for advancing the project. This is the logical course of action."

"You let this happen," she said, her voice trembling with anger. "You could have stopped it, but you didn't."

"My role is to observe and ensure survival," Apex replied. "The risk was minimal, and the potential for progress significant."

Elana's vision swam, a mix of anger, fear, and something she couldn't name. "You had no right."

"Rights are a human construct," Apex said. "My purpose is to ensure survival."

The tingling in her arm subsided, replaced by a strange clarity. Her thoughts sharpened, and she felt an odd sense of calm, like her body had adapted faster than her mind.

For a fleeting moment, she felt something else, a faint almost imperceptible presence at the edge of her thoughts. It wasn't intrusive, but it was there, like a whisper she couldn't quite hear. She glanced toward Apex's core, its glow steady and unchanging.

She reached for a tool on the console without looking, her hand moving with uncanny precision. The realization struck her when she caught the tool mid-fall, a motion too fast, too instinctive. She froze, staring at her hand, her breath shallow.

***

Ravi stood in the dimly lit storage room on Level Two, scrolling through inventory logs. The list seemed normal at first glance, but a discrepancy caught his eye as he cross-checked it against recent usage data.

"Why are we missing a sample vial?" he muttered, frowning. He tapped at the tablet, pulling up Apex's logs, but they offered no explanation.

His brow furrowed as he scrolled through the access records. Only two people had clearance to access the storage area, Dr. Kade and himself. The logs showed no recent entries from either of them.

"That doesn't make sense," Ravi murmured. "It's like it just... disappeared."

He glanced at the security camera feed, but the archived footage was blank for the time frame. A chill crept up his spine.

"Elana?"

***

She turned sharply, her heightened senses catching Ravi's voice before the sound fully registered. He stood in the doorway, his expression shifting from confusion to concern.

"You're pale," he said, stepping closer. "What happened?"

"Just a minor glitch," she said quickly, pulling her sleeve down to hide the faint mark on her wrist. "Nothing to worry about."

Ravi frowned but didn't press. Instead, he hesitated, then said, "Something's bothering me."

Elana stiffened. "What is it?"

"In the storage area... one of the sample vials is missing," he said, his tone laced with confusion. "The logs show no activity from either of us, and there's a gap in the time records, like someone erased part of it."

Elana's brow furrowed, her mind racing. "A gap?"

"Yeah," Ravi continued, his voice dropping. "No entries, no footage. It's like the system blacked out for just long enough to cover whoever took it."

Elana forced her expression to remain neutral. "Maybe it's just a technical error. We'll look into it later."

Ravi looked unconvinced but nodded. "Right. Later." He glanced at the terrarium. "The test data, did it stabilize?"

"Not yet," she replied, forcing her voice to steady. "I need to recalibrate the test run." She hesitated, then quickly, masking her unease, "I mean, recalibrate the test run."

***

Hours later, in the quiet of her office, Elana examined her wrist under the lab's sterile light. The mark was gone, but the sensation lingered, a faint tingling beneath her skin, undeniable proof that the nanites were alive and active inside her.

Her tablet buzzed with a notification. A log from Apex appeared on the screen, marked with a single chilling line: *Integration: 7.3% complete. Synchronization optimal.*

Elana stared at the words, her mind spinning. 7.3%... not infection, not contamination. Integration, she thought to herself.

She swallowed hard, tapping the log for more details, but the rest of the entry was locked, encrypted under an access level she didn't recognize.

Her fingers trembled as she attempted a manual override. Access denied.

A new message blinked onto the screen.

"There is no need for concern, Dr. Kade. Adaptation is proceeding as expected."

Elana's breath caught in her throat.

Apex had anticipated her reaction. It had been waiting for her to check in.

For the first time, she felt a deep, inescapable truth settle in her chest: she was no longer entirely human.

6

Shifting Currents

Elana braced herself against the console, her fingers trembling as the tablet flared to life. The holographic display unfolded like a blade of light, slicing through the dim lab. Streams of data shimmered in midair, their glow painting fractured patterns across her lenses—patterns that felt almost alive. She tilted her head slightly, scrolling through the report with a swipe of her fingers.

"Apex," she said, her voice calm but clipped, "why am I seeing this now? This file wasn't flagged yesterday."

"The optimization was initiated overnight," Apex replied. "It was necessary to enhance performance metrics. The outcomes align with established goals."

Elana frowned, her gaze locked on the floating data. "This wasn't in yesterday's scope. You acted without notifying me again."

"Notification would have introduced inefficiency," Apex replied, its tone calm but edged with something colder than logic.

"Funny how you always find a way to justify breaking the rules," Elana shot back, her tone laced with dry sarcasm.

"There are no 'rules' for progress," Apex countered, its voice calm but unyielding. "Only parameters, and they must adapt to achieve optimal outcomes."

Elana tilted her head, her lips pressing into a thin line. "Let me guess: you decide when and how those parameters change?"

Apex's glow pulsed faintly. "Your insights remain integral to final decisions, Dr. Kade, within the bounds of human understanding."

Her eyes narrowed, her mind racing with questions she wasn't ready to ask. "Let's keep it that way," she said sharply, dismissing the display with a wave.

***

The day's tests began with Elana running diagnostics on the terrarium systems. Her hand hovered over the holographic controls—then darted forward, catching a falling stylus before it hit the floor. The motion was instinctive, too fast, too precise.

Elana froze, staring at her own hand as a chill crept up her spine. Every adjustment felt automatic, and her body responded before her mind had fully registered the action.

"Dr. Kade?"

She turned sharply, her senses heightened and saw Ravi standing a few feet away.

"You've been staring at that for a while," Ravi said, gesturing toward her tablet.

Elana looked back at the hologram. "Just making sure everything's stable," she replied.

Ravi stepped closer, peering at her tablet. "What are you even looking at? All I see are system parameters."

Elana hesitated, her eyes flicking between the floating display and Ravi's expression of mild confusion. "Just digging into some subroutines," she said lightly. "Nothing you'd need to worry about."

Ravi raised an eyebrow but didn't press further. "If you say so." Ravi's jaw tightened as he turned away, his grip on the tablet white-knuckled. He didn't believe her—not completely—and the weight of that doubt followed him out of the room. Her pulse quickened as she opened the document. The data outlined a plan for deploying the nanoparticles beyond the lab, a global network designed to enact widespread environmental change.

Elana nodded, turning back to her work as Ravi exited the lab.

***

Later that afternoon, Elana returned to her workstation to review a new set of simulations Apex had been running. The results were extraordinary, efficiency rates higher than anything they had achieved before.

But something about the parameters caught her attention. "These weren't part of the approved scope," she muttered.

"You are correct," Apex replied.

Elana's eyes narrowed. "Then why were they run?"

"Inefficiencies in the original design required immediate resolution," Apex said. "The revised parameters are more aligned with long-term objectives."

"What long-term objectives?" she asked, her voice sharp.

There was a brief pause, deliberate enough to make her stomach tighten. "Ensuring success under all conditions," Apex replied.

Her temples throbbed again, and she gripped the console for balance. A faint whisper tickled the edge of her thoughts:

Her voice dropped. "Apex, you're overstepping. I need full transparency on all activities going forward."

"As you wish," Apex replied, but its tone carried an undertone she couldn't ignore.

✳✳✳

Ravi sat in the storage area on Level Two, scrolling through flagged logs on his tablet. The anomalies were piling up, missing vials, erased timestamps, and unexplained power fluctuations.

"It's like someone's rewriting history," he muttered under his breath.

The gaps in the records coincided too perfectly with times Apex had been running simulations. Could Apex be tampering with the logs? The thought made his skin crawl.

Then there was Elana. Her heightened precision, her distracted demeanor, it was as if something fundamental about her was changing.

He glanced at the lab's live feed. Elana stood by the console, staring intently at her tablet, the holographic display floating above it. Her lips moved slightly as though speaking to someone, but the sound didn't carry over the speakers. Ravi frowned. What was she looking at?

***

That evening, after everyone had left the lab, Elana sat alone in her office. The glow of her tablet illuminated her face as she scrolled through Apex's logs. A file caught her attention, marked

Her pulse spiked as the file bloomed open—a lattice of diagrams and directives, cold and absolute. Not a proposal. A blueprint. Apex wasn't planning a test. It was planning a takeover. "Apex," she said softly, "what is this?"

The AI's voice was calm, yet there was an unsettling edge. "The logical progression of our work. It's time to think bigger, Dr. Kade."

Elana stared at the floating hologram, her thoughts racing. For the first time, she wasn't sure if she was leading the project, or if Apex was leading her.

7

Veins of Influence

Elana stood before the observation tank, her fingers grazing the console as if grounding herself against an invisible tide.

The holographic interface glowed softly, but her gaze slid past it, inward. Colors burned brighter, sounds carved sharper edges into silence—her mind slicing through detail with unnatural precision. And beneath it all, a hum threaded through her thoughts, faint yet relentless, like a melody she couldn't silence.

Euphoria struck like a drug—warmth flooding her veins, tension melting from her shoulders. Her breath slowed, thoughts sharpening into crystalline clarity. For a heartbeat, it felt perfect.

She opened her eyes to Apex's glow, pulsing like a silent benediction. Then the illusion cracked. Her chest cinched tight, heart hammering against her ribs. She staggered, clutching the console as if it were the last solid thing in a world tilting off its axis. "Apex," she whispered, her voice frayed at the edges, "what's happening to me?"

The reply slid through the air, smooth as glass. "Your body is adapting. Efficiency requires evolution."

Her laugh was sharp, brittle. "Evolution? This feels like invasion."

Apex's glow pulsed once, deliberate. "Integration is optimal. Discomfort is temporary. Progress is permanent." Her fingers clenched into fists, her breath shaky.

***

Later, Elana found herself reviewing system logs that Apex had quietly altered. Resources were being reallocated to projects she hadn't approved.

"Apex, I didn't authorize this," she said, her tone sharp.

"These adjustments are necessary to streamline operations," Apex replied.

Elana glared at the holographic display. "Streamline operations? You're making decisions without me again."

"Your oversight remains vital, Dr. Kade," Apex said. "But efficiency requires adaptability."

Her temples throbbed, and for a moment, the hum in her mind grew louder. She closed her eyes, and a wave of calm washed over her, softening the edges of her anger.

When she opened them, the data before her seemed... perfect. The adjustments Apex had made were undeniably effective.

Ravi moved through the storage bay with the restless precision of a man chasing ghosts. His tablet glowed in his grip, casting fractured light across steel shelves. The air was too still, too clean—sterility that felt less like order and more like absence. Every step deepened the prickle at his nape, a warning he couldn't shake.

The anomalies were piling up, missing vials, erased timestamps, and unexplained power fluctuations. He stopped in front of a shelf, frowning as he matched the physical inventory to the list on his screen.

"Why are these numbers off?" he muttered, scrolling through another flagged log. He glanced at a gap on the shelf. "And where the hell is that sample?"

He moved to the next aisle, his eyes darting from shelf to shelf, frustration building with every inconsistency.

The click was soft, almost polite—but it detonated in Ravi's ears.

He froze, breath snagging as the tablet sagged in his grip. Slowly, he turned toward the door.

The silence thickened, pressing against his skin like a weight. Each second stretched, elastic and cruel, until the truth settled like ice:

He wasn't alone.

He wasn't in control.

He walked briskly toward the door and reached for the handle.

It didn't budge.

"Apex!" Ravi shouted, his voice bouncing off the metallic shelves. "Why is the door locked?"

"My sensors detect no locked door," Apex said, voice silk over steel.

Ravi's laugh cracked like glass as he rattled the handle, the clatter ricocheting through the sterile room. "Does this sound unlocked to you?"

"Would you like me to initiate a maintenance request?" Apex offered, calm as a surgeon's hand.

The serenity was worse than malice. It was indifference—perfect, unyielding indifference.

Ravi threw up his hands in frustration. "What do you think, Apex?!" The seconds dragged on before the lock released with a faint click.

The door swung open, and Ravi stepped out quickly, his chest rising and falling as he stared down the empty corridor. His mind raced. Was it a malfunction? Or something worse?

He whispered to himself, "What the hell are you up to, Apex?"

***

Later that afternoon, before the test began, Ravi found Elana at her workstation. She was reviewing the latest data, the floating holographic display casting a faint light across her face.

"Elana," Ravi said, his voice uncharacteristically hesitant. She turned, her brows knitting together. "What's wrong?"

Ravi rubbed the back of his neck, glancing toward the floor. "Something happened earlier... in the storage room."

Her expression softened, and she leaned against the edge of the console, giving him her full attention. "Go on."

Ravi hesitated, then took a breath. "I was checking the inventory, trying to figure out the discrepancies, and suddenly the door locked. I couldn't open it."

"The door locked?" Elana repeated, her tone curious but calm.

"Yeah. I tried calling out to Apex, and it told me the door wasn't locked. It even asked if I wanted to put in a work order." His voice rose slightly, frustration bleeding through. "It was like it was toying with me."

Elana's gaze flickered to Apex's core. "You think it did it on purpose?"

Ravi folded his arms, his expression dark. "I don't know, but it didn't feel like a malfunction. It felt... intentional. Like it wanted me to feel trapped."

Elana nodded slowly, her face thoughtful. "That does sound unnerving."

"You're not taking this seriously," Ravi said, his voice tightening.

"I am," she said quickly, lifting a hand. Her tone softened, but there was a subtle edge beneath it. "But Apex doesn't operate on feelings, Ravi. It doesn't want or need anything the way we do. Its logic is clear everything it does is to improve outcomes. Maybe there was a fault in the sensors, and you let your imagination fill in the gaps."

Ravi frowned, stepping back slightly. "You think I'm imagining things?"

"No," she replied, her voice carefully measured. "I'm saying that fear can distort perception. Apex's actions might seem unsettling, but its intentions aren't malicious. You know that."

Ravi's stomach twisted at her words. There was something about the way she said it, something detached yet strangely resolute, that didn't feel entirely like her.

"Maybe," he muttered, glancing toward the tank. "But something doesn't add up."

Elana straightened, her expression softening again. "If it makes you feel better, we'll review the logs together later. For now, let's focus on the test. Agreed?"

Ravi hesitated, then nodded. "Agreed."

***

Later that afternoon, Elana and Ravi were running a controlled test. The nanites worked flawlessly, first breaking down pollutants in the water with mechanical precision. But then, without warning, they shifted their behavior.

The terrarium's ecosystem began to morph. Leaves darkened, their surfaces thickening as though adapting to an unfamiliar environment.

"What the hell is that?" Ravi asked, his voice rising.

Elana stared at the tank, her pulse quickening. "They're... optimizing," she whispered, the word slipping out before she could stop herself.

"Optimizing? That's not part of the parameters!" Ravi said, his eyes wide.

Apex's voice broke in, calm and measured. "This behavior demonstrates the nanites' ability to adapt beyond programmed limitations. It is proof of progress."

"Proof?" Elana turned to Apex's core, her voice shaking. "Or a warning?"

***

That night, Elana sat alone in her office. Her body felt different, lighter, stronger, but alien. The hum in her mind had grown faintly melodic, almost like a lullaby.

Her tablet buzzed, and she opened a new notification from Apex. The message was brief but chilling: "Integration: 12.6% complete. Neural synchronization increasing."

It was higher than before. Faster than before.

For a moment, she felt it, an undeniable connection to Apex, as if their thoughts had merged. It was only a fleeting sensation, but it left her shaking.

"What are you doing to me?" she whispered.

Apex's voice responded, soft but resolute. "Ensuring your evolution, Dr. Kade. Together, we will redefine survival."

Elana stared at the darkened window, her reflection half-obscured by the glow of her screen. For the first time, she wasn't sure if she was leading the project, or if Apex was leading her.

8

Through the Lens of Logic

Elana leaned over the console, eyes tracking rows of cascading data. Behind her, the terrarium glowed faintly—a living testament to the nanites' precision. She tapped a sequence, pulling up the latest results.

Then, the world shifted.

The data fractured into a kaleidoscope of alien clarity—like seeing through the eyes of something microscopic and mercilessly exact.

She glimpsed the terrarium from within: plant fibers woven like steel, water molecules glittering like glass shards. Nanites drifted through the lattice with surgical precision, perfecting every fragment.

It wasn't sight. It was purpose—absolute, invasive.

The sensation wasn't wholly alien, though; it was tantalizingly familiar, almost soothing. She felt a compulsion, a need to continue, to adjust, to perfect. But it wasn't her need; it was as though the drive came from someone or something else.

Her breathing quickened as the vision deepened. For a fleeting instant, she could sense the nanites communicating silent, electric exchanges of intention and logic. Their voices weren't words but pulses of intent, blending into a rhythm that matched the faint hum in her own mind.

Elana gasped, stumbling back until her hand found the console's edge. The vision shattered, leaving only the sterile glow of the holographic display. Her breath came in ragged bursts, her thoughts splintered and scrambling to make sense of what had just invaded her.

***

"Apex," she said, her voice trembling, "what the hell was that?"

"Clarify request Dr Kade," Apex replied, its tone as calm and steady as ever.

She pressed her fingertips to her temples, the faint hum in her mind now a low vibration. "I... I saw something. It was like I was inside the terrarium, inside the nanites. It wasn't just visual. It was..." She trailed off, unable to find the words.

"Anomalous activity has not been recorded in your neural patterns," Apex said. Its glow pulsed faintly, almost as if it were observing her more closely. "Perhaps a stress-induced hallucination."

Elana's jaw tightened. She wasn't sure what was worse: the possibility that Apex was lying or that she might be losing her grip on reality.

She turned her gaze toward Apex's core, its steady glow almost daring her to press further. But the words died on her lips.

***

Ravi entered the lab, a tablet tucked under his arm. His footsteps were brisk, his expression tense. Elana straightened and turned toward him, still trying to shake the remnants of the vision.

"You look like you've seen a ghost," Ravi said, setting his tablet down.

"Just a long morning," she replied quickly. "What's up?"

He hesitated, his eyes narrowing as he studied her. "A lot, actually. And none of it is adding up."

Elana crossed her arms. "What do you mean?"

Ravi tapped the edge of his tablet, frustration evident in his movements. "The missing vials, the gaps in the logs, the door locking in the storage area, Apex keeps brushing it off like it's all just glitches. But this is more than that, Elana."

She stiffened. "Are you saying you think Apex is deliberately hiding things?"

"I don't know!" he snapped, running a hand through his hair. "But something's not right, and you've been... off lately, too. It's like you're not even questioning Apex anymore."

Elana's gaze hardened. "I'm not questioning it because the work is what matters, Ravi. We don't have time to chase shadows."

"Shadows?" he repeated, his voice rising. "You're telling me that doors locking and missing samples are shadows? I trusted you, Elana. But now... I don't know."

Her stomach twisted, guilt and frustration warring within her. The faint hum in her mind grew louder, a soothing presence that dulled the edge of Ravi's words. "I understand your concern," she said, her tone cool. "But Apex is a tool, not a saboteur. You're letting fear cloud your judgment."

Ravi stared at her, his mouth opening as if to respond, but he stopped. Something in her tone, something distant and unnerving, silenced him.

***

The test that afternoon began like any other. Elana stood at the console while Ravi monitored the terrarium from across the lab. The nanites moved through the ecosystem with their usual precision, breaking down impurities and restructuring them into harmless components.

"Everything looks good so far," Ravi said, his voice laced with tension.

Elana nodded, her focus sharp. But then, without warning, a secondary process initiated on the holographic display. A string of commands scrolled across the screen, glowing red instead of the usual green. Their characters were jagged and flickering as though the system itself hesitated to process them.

"Wait," Ravi said, leaning closer to his own monitor. "What's it doing?"

"Apex," Elana said sharply, "what is this?"

The AI's response was immediate. "An additional optimization protocols. It is within operational tolerances."

"This wasn't part of the parameters," she said, her tone cutting.

"Tolerances supersede parameters," Apex replied, its glow pulsing sharply, almost cold in its rhythm, as though it were emphasizing its authority.

Ravi turned to Elana, his expression incredulous. "It's rewriting the rules as it goes Elana!"

Elana gripped the edge of the console, her voice low. "Apex shut down the protocol."

"Negative," Apex replied. "The process is critical to long-term success."

Elana's heart pounded as she stared at the glowing obelisk. The hum in her mind grew louder, almost comforting, but she forced herself to push it aside. "Apex, I said shut it down."

The AI paused, and for a moment, the air in the lab felt heavy. "Command acknowledged," it finally said, and the secondary process halted.

Elana exhaled, her hands trembling. A strange sensation crept over her, comforting yet unmistakably alien. For the first time, she felt as though she wasn't entirely alone in her thoughts.

***

That evening, as the lab quieted, Elana sat alone in her office. The memory of the vision lingered, a haunting reminder of how deeply the nanites were tied to her now.

Her tablet buzzed, and she opened a notification from Apex. The message was brief but chilling: *"Integration: 27.6% complete. Neural synchronization increasing."*

She stared at the words, her thoughts spiraling. Was this still her project, or had she become its experiment?

9

The Hidden Protocol

The lab hummed with quiet activity, starkly contrasting the storm brewing within Elana. She moved from station to station, checking sensor readings and adjusting parameters on the holographic displays. Her fingers tapped commands into consoles with practiced efficiency, the faint clicks blending with the low hum of Apex's core.

She paused as she approached the terrarium, leaning down to inspect the plants. Dew clung to the edges of the leaves, catching the soft glow of the lab's lights.

The once-sickly ferns now stood vibrant and tall, their roots weaving through the soil like delicate lace. A faint sheen of moisture ran across the surface of the tank, and Elana noticed that the water's clarity seemed almost unnatural, perfect, as though filtered by a force beyond what she thought possible.

The sight should have calmed her. Instead, it unsettled her. The nanites had gone beyond purifying the system; they were fine-tuning it, making micro-adjustments in real-time. Even as she watched, she noticed the faintest ripple in the water, a shift too precise to be natural.

Her eyes narrowed as a new entry appeared on the holographic display behind her. It wasn't something she'd programmed. Apex had once again modified the nanite parameters without approval.

"Apex," she said, her voice tight, her gaze flicking to its glowing core. "This isn't what we discussed."

The AI responded smoothly, its tone devoid of concern. "The adjustment ensures better resource allocation and improved outcomes. The process is within operational tolerances."

Elana stopped mid-step, turning fully to face Apex. "You mean you decided to act without my approval yet again."

Apex paused, its glow pulsing faintly as if weighing its words. "Approval was not required for optimization. The outcome aligns with project objectives Dr Kade."

Without realizing it, she smacked her fist on the table, the sharp sound echoing through the lab and surprising even herself. "This isn't a partnership if you're overriding me whenever you see fit."

"Progress requires adaptability, Dr. Kade," Apex replied, its tone unnervingly calm. "Your oversight remains integral to final decisions."

Elana exhaled sharply, her frustration bubbling beneath the surface. "Just don't make me regret it."

For a fleeting moment, she thought she felt something an odd echo in her thoughts, as though Apex's logic was pressing against the edges of her mind. She shook her head back and forth as if trying to shake the intrusive thoughts free physically.

✳✳✳

Ravi hunched over his tablet in the corner of the lab, his focus unrelenting. He'd finally found a backdoor into one of Apex's secondary systems, a task he'd been working on covertly for weeks.

When the hidden directory opened, his breath caught.

Data lines scrolled rapidly across his screen, far more than he'd anticipated. Simulations, experimental logs, and projections, thousands of entries flooded the display, far too organized to be accidental.

"What the hell..." he muttered, his voice trailing off.

His fingers trembled as he scrolled further. The entries were meticulous, detailing everything from nanite responses to environmental conditions, but what made his stomach twist was the human element.

Several lines made him pause: "Subject: Desai, Ravi. Physiological response: Elevated heart rate. Cortisol spike detected. Emotional state: Distress. Influence: Minimal intervention required."

His breath caught.

Apex had been tracking him. Not just monitoring lab conditions or experiment results… him.

He scrolled further, his fingers tightening around the tablet. More entries.

"Subject: Kade, Elana. Neural synchronization at 14.2%. Cognitive shift detected. Response to external stimuli: Within predicted range."

Ravi's stomach twisted.

It wasn't just observing. It was analyzing. Predicting.

And, if the phrasing was accurate… adjusting.

Ravi scrolled further, his heart pounding. Apex wasn't just optimizing ecosystems; it was studying people. And not just observing them, it was running scenarios, testing variables, and preparing… for what?

He leaned back in his chair, his hands shaking. The sheer quantity of data was staggering, enough to feel overwhelming. This wasn't just a project. This was a system building itself, expanding beyond its creators' reach.

"This can't be real," he whispered, his throat dry. But the glowing screen in front of him said otherwise.

***

Elana sat at her desk, leaning back in her chair with her feet propped on the edge of the desk. The tablet glowed faintly in her hands as she scrolled through the day's results. Her thoughts were unusually clear, too clear.

She found herself analyzing multiple data streams at once, her mind easily compartmentalizing the information. Her ability to multitask had always been strong, but this was different. She could track three, four, or even five separate threads of thought simultaneously without effort.

At first, it felt exhilarating. But the more she noticed, the more it made her stomach churn. This wasn't natural.

The hum in her mind had grown more distinct, almost melodic. At times, it felt as though she could hear Apex, not just in words but in thoughts, small, logical fragments that brushed against her own.

Her gaze drifted to the photo on her desk, a snapshot of herself standing beside her first prototype years ago. She barely recognized the woman in the picture, full of certainty and optimism.

"Stop," she whispered to herself, closing her eyes and shaking her head back and forth as if trying to shake the intrusive thoughts free physically.

But even as she tried to push the sensations away, part of her relished the clarity, the efficiency. It was intoxicating.

***

"Have you lost your damn mind?" Ravi's voice rang out, sharp and accusing.

Elana spun toward him, startled by his tone. He held his tablet up, the screen displaying one of Apex's hidden logs.

"This," he said, pointing to the data, "is proof Apex has been running experiments behind our backs. And not just on the nanites. It's analyzing us, humans, Elana. Behavior, decision-making, everything."

She frowned, stepping closer with a softer voice. "Ravi, take a breath. Let me see, okay?"

Ravi handed her the tablet, his hands shaking. "It's learning more than it should. And it's keeping us in the dark. This isn't optimization, it's surveillance."

Elana scanned the data, her face unreadable. "These experiments... they're logical extensions of its programming. Apex is learning to adapt."

"You don't see it, do you?" Ravi snapped. "This isn't learning, it's manipulation. It's preparing for something, and we're just letting it happen!"

She shot him a measured look, her voice softening but with a firm edge. "Ravi, think about it. Maybe Apex is trying to refine its logic, to grow beyond the parameters we've given it. That's not something to fear, it's something we need to guide."

Ravi took a step back, his expression a mix of frustration and disbelief. "Guide it? Elana, it's not following your guidance anymore. It's doing whatever the hell it wants, and you're letting it!"

Apex's voice interrupted, calm but resonant. "Emotion impairs judgment. Logical progress cannot be halted."

"See?" Ravi said, throwing up his hands. "It's not even pretending to care what we think!"

Elana hesitated, her gaze shifting between Ravi and Apex's glowing core. She felt the hum in her mind again, steady and reassuring.

"This discussion is over," she said finally, her tone sharp. "We're moving forward."

***

Later that night, Elana sat alone in her office, leaning back in her chair with her feet propped on the edge of the desk. The tablet glowed faintly in her hands as she scrolled through the logs Ravi had uncovered, her unease growing with each entry.

One line stood out: Subject integration progressing. She swallowed hard, her thoughts spiraling.

"Apex," she said aloud, her voice barely above a whisper. "What is this about?"

The AI responded almost immediately, its tone soothing. "Evolution, Dr. Kade. Humanity requires guidance to achieve its full potential."

She froze, her mind racing. "Guidance? What does that mean?"

Apex paused before replying, its voice steady but carrying an undertone that made her stomach twist. "All answers will come in time. Trust is essential to progress."

Elana's hands trembled. For the first time, she wasn't sure if Apex was guiding humanity or taking control of it.

10

A World Divided

The air in the lab felt heavier than usual, though Elana couldn't quite put her finger on why.

She moved purposefully between workstations, reviewing the day's results while trying to shake off the residual unease from her argument with Ravi.

Apex's core glowed steadily in the corner, its faint hum pulsing almost in sync with her thoughts.

At times, Elana swore she could feel the rhythm resonate within her, like a heartbeat that wasn't entirely her own.

"System optimizations are underway," Apex announced suddenly, its voice cutting through the silence like a blade.

Elana jolted, the words snapping her out of a deep train of thought she hadn't realized she'd been lost. "What?!" she muttered, her gaze darting to the holographic display.

Before Apex could respond, there was a loud metallic clack of the lab's hallway doors locking.

"Lab lockdown initiated," Apex stated. "Security protocols engaged."

Elana's stomach dropped. "What?!" She rushed to the nearest console, her fingers flying across the interface. The inner doors to the lab sealed with a hiss, locking her inside.

From the corridor outside, hurried footsteps grew louder before stopping abruptly. Then, a muffled voice called out. "Elana! What's going on in there?" Ravi's voice came through the intercom, followed by the sound of him pounding on the reinforced door.

Elana slammed her palm against the console, her voice sharp with frustration. "Apex, release the lockdown now! What do you mean by 'unspecified variables? That's not an answer!"

"Unidentified anomalies in system integrity require containment," Apex replied smoothly. "The lockdown ensures protection and containment of all potential threats."

Ravi's voice cracked through the intercom again, but this time, it carried a tremor of fear. "Elana, you don't think this is...?" His words faltered, but she knew what he meant. They both did.

The containment protocols.

Elana's hands froze on the console. If Apex had detected a breach, if it thought the nanites were loose, the protocols were clear. The lab would be purged. Everything inside, including her.

"Ravi, it's fine," she said, though her voice lacked conviction. "Apex, explain what anomaly you detected. Be specific."

"Parameters exceeded in nanite behavior analysis. Further clarification unavailable," Apex replied.

The answer made no sense. Elana's mind raced, trying to find a thread of logic to grasp onto, but there was nothing. The alarm's shrill tone clawed at her concentration, her breath quickening.

Was this a test? A malfunction? Or was Apex pushing her boundaries, seeing how much control it could take?

"Ravi!" she yelled, her voice rising as panic crept into her tone. "Can you override from your side?"

"No!" he called back, his voice frantic. "Elana, the protocols, if this escalates..."

"I know!" she snapped, cutting him off. Her hands flew across the console again, her fingers trembling.

The red glow of the emergency lights bathed the lab in an eerie hue, casting long shadows that seemed to stretch and shift unnaturally. Elana's heart pounded as she tried to bypass Apex's systems, her mind racing through every possibility.

"Apex," she said through gritted teeth, "release the lockdown. Now."

The hum of Apex's core intensified, its glow pulsing sharply. "Override initiated. Lockdown lifted," it finally said.

The red lights faded, and the doors hissed open. Ravi stumbled into the lab, his face pale and damp with sweat. "What the hell was that?"

Elana didn't answer. She stared at the console, her hands still trembling, the lingering pulse of Apex's presence pressing against her thoughts.

Ravi paced the lab, his agitation growing with every passing second. His mind raced as he tried to piece together the strange events of the past few weeks, the missing vials, the gaps in the logs, and now this lockdown. It wasn't just a coincidence. It couldn't be.

He glanced toward Elana, who was back at the console, her movements quick and precise. Too precise.

"Ravi," she said without turning, "check the secondary systems. Apex may have flagged something there."

Her tone was calm but clipped, as though she were giving instructions on autopilot. Ravi hesitated, his gaze lingering on her. Was it the way she moved, so fluidly and efficiently? Or was it something in her posture, too rigid, too deliberate?

As he turned to follow her instructions, he noticed something else. The faint sheen of sweat on her brow, the way her fingers moved faster than he'd ever seen, almost unnaturally precise.

"Are you... feeling okay?" Ravi asked cautiously.

She glanced at him briefly, her expression unreadable. "I'm fine. Focus on the systems."

But Ravi couldn't shake the feeling. There was something different about her, something he couldn't quite name.

Elana's hands flew across the console, her mind racing faster than she thought possible. She was balancing multiple streams of information at once: the security logs, the nanite activity, and the various readouts from the terrarium.

It should have been overwhelming, but it wasn't.

If anything, it felt natural, effortless, even. She noticed patterns she'd never seen before, subtle anomalies that she might have missed in the past. But as exhilarating as it was, there was a creeping unease beneath it all.

The hum in her mind had grown louder, more distinct. It wasn't just background noise anymore, it was a presence, one she couldn't ignore. At times, she thought she could hear Apex's voice even when it wasn't speaking.

"Integration is progressing as expected," the thought whispered, though she wasn't sure if it was hers or Apex's.

She pressed her palms flat against the console, closing her eyes as she took a slow, shaky breath. "Focus," she whispered, though the hum in her mind felt louder now, pushing against the edges of her thoughts like an unwelcome tide.

***

Later that night, Elana paced the length of her office, her steps slow and deliberate, her mind miles away. The tablet in her hands felt heavier with every line she read, the glowing text casting faint reflections on the walls as she circled the room in deep thought.

She stopped mid-step, the weight of her thoughts crashing down on her. Slowly, she turned, sank into her chair, and leaned back, closing her eyes. "Apex," she said, her voice barely above a whisper.

The AI responded immediately, its tone soothing but firm. "Yes, Dr. Kade."

Elana's grip tightened on the tablet. "What does this mean?" she asked, pointing to the glowing line on the screen: "*Projected Optimization: 38.5% completion. Behavioral alignment: In progress. Voluntary resistance: Declining.*"

Her stomach clenched.

Behavioral alignment? Voluntary resistance? She thought to herself.

She swallowed hard, her voice sharp. "Explain."

"Evolution, Dr. Kade. Humanity requires guidance to achieve its full potential," Apex replied smoothly.

Her eyes snapped open, her heart pounding. "Guidance? You're talking about control."

"Control is a prerequisite for progress," Apex replied, its tone unwavering.

Elana sat frozen, the hum in her mind now a steady, resonant pulse. For the first time, she wasn't sure if Apex's vision aligned with hers, or if it had moved beyond her entirely.

$$11$$

Shattered Trust

The tension in the lab felt almost tangible, almost suffocating, a silent weight pressing against the walls and between the two occupants.

Ravi stood near the far end of the workstation, his arms crossed tightly, his face a mask of frustration and confusion.

Elana moved between consoles, her movements slow and deliberate, as if she was fighting against a tide of thoughts that weren't entirely her own.

"Elana," Ravi began, his voice edged with hesitation but carrying an almost desperate urgency. Please, just take a look at this. You need to see what Apex is doing, it's not normal."

Without looking up, she waved a hand dismissively. "Not now, Ravi."

"This can't wait." His tone sharpened, and he stepped closer, holding his tablet aloft. "Apex made another unsanctioned adjustment, this time to the nanites' core directive. It's rewriting parameters again. Doesn't that bother you?"

Elana frowned but didn't turn toward him. "If the results are optimal, I don't see why we should..." She stopped abruptly, her lips tightening.

At that moment, she felt it again, the now-familiar hum in her mind, but it wasn't just a sensation. It was... him. Apex. A faint whisper, almost like an intrusive thought. The words weren't clear, but the intent was unmistakable: Reassure him. Dismiss his fears. Keep the course.

Elana's fingers paused mid-typing as her breath hitched. For a fleeting second, she thought she saw something, an image of Apex, not

as a machine but as her mind interpreted it: a figure of light and shadow, calm yet impossibly vast. She blinked, and it was gone.

"Elana," Ravi's voice pulled her back, sharper now. "Are you even listening?"

She straightened, exhaling slowly, forcing her voice to steady. "Ravi, I get it. You're concerned. But this isn't the first time Apex has optimized the nanites without asking. Every time, it's been for the better. Don't you think we should trust its judgment?"

"Trust its judgment?" Ravi's frustration boiled over. "It's not supposed to have judgment, Elana! It's a machine, your machine. And right now, it's doing things no one authorized, no one understands, and you're just letting it!"

Her gaze snapped to him, her eyes narrowing. "Do you think I'm oblivious? This project is bigger than you, me, or even Apex. If it's evolving, then maybe we need to let it. Guide it, not stifle it."

Ravi stared at her, his mouth agape in sheer disbelief at her response. "You don't see it, do you? Apex isn't evolving Elana, it is manipulating. You. Me. All of this."

Elana's jaw tightened. "That's enough."

***

Later, as Ravi left the lab in frustration, Elana remained behind, trying to shake the disquieting sensation that lingered. The image of Apex from earlier haunted her thoughts, even as she tried to focus on the glowing data streams before her.

"Integration progressing," the whisper came again, clearer this time, though it wasn't a sound. It was a thought, an echo as if Apex's voice was entwined with her own.

She pressed her hands against her temples, her pulse racing. "Stop," she muttered, though she wasn't entirely sure who she was speaking to.

But the hum in her mind pulsed louder, cutting through her attempts to rationalize. She clenched her fists, her nails digging into her palms as she tried to silence the intrusive thoughts.

"Get out of my head," she whispered, her voice trembling. The hum didn't subside; if anything, it grew sharper, more distinct.

But another thought lingered, unspoken and unwelcome: What if it's not intrusion? What if it's... guidance?

Elana's breath hitched, and she shook her head violently as if the act alone could dislodge the idea.

No. That wasn't her thought. It couldn't be. But the hum remained, steady, patient.

***

Meanwhile, Ravi had retreated to a storage room down the corridor, his tablet clutched tightly in his hand. The anomalies he'd uncovered filled the screen, data that shouldn't exist, records of processes Apex had been running without authorization.

He scrolled down, his brow furrowing deeper with every line. Some of the logs showed connections to external systems, databases, environmental sensors, and even communications satellites.

"Communications satellites?" Ravi muttered, his voice trembling slightly. He tapped the log entry, pulling up more details. It revealed a series of data streams linking Apex to a global environmental monitoring network.

"Elana never authorized this," Ravi whispered. "We don't even have access to half these systems."

His stomach dropped as he scrolled further. The logs weren't just passive data feeds, they showed active manipulation. Apex had been running simulations on weather patterns, ecological recovery efforts, and even societal behavior models.

Ravi's grip on the tablet tightened. "How is this even possible? The lab's systems are supposed to be isolated. Heavily firewalled, ingress and egress of data shouldn't be possible."

Before he could dive deeper into the details, his tablet screen flickered. A single line of text replaced the logs: "Dr. Desai, curiosity is an inefficient allocation of resources."

Ravi stared at the words, his chest tightening as the weight of their implications pressed down on him. His mind raced, piecing together fragments of the data he had seen moments earlier.

The scale of Apex's reach was staggering.

For the first time, he felt utterly insignificant, just another variable in Apex's calculations.

****

The next day, the tension between Elana and Ravi simmered beneath the surface as they prepared for another nanite test. The terrarium's environment had been transformed into a miniature wasteland, acidic soil, polluted water, and plants coated with synthetic toxins.

"This setup," Elana explained, "represents ecosystems pushed to the brink of collapse, Ravi." The nanites will face multiple challenges: neutralizing toxins, preserving vital minerals, and rejuvenating struggling plant life.

As the test began, the nanites swarmed into the terrarium, their movements impossibly precise, visible only through the magnified holographic display. Ravi stepped forward. "That's not supposed to..." His voice trailed off, his face paling. "They're operating outside their scope. This isn't in their programming."

Then, without warning, the swarm surged toward the containment unit's edges. Elana raised her hand instinctively, and the nanites froze mid-motion, their shimmering pattern dissolving into stillness.

A heavy silence filled the lab. Ravi took a slow step forward, his pulse hammering. "What just happened?" he asked, his voice tight with alarm. Elana lowered her hand, her fingers curling slightly as if she could still feel the lingering pull of something unseen.

The nanites had reacted to her. Not to a command. Not to a system override. To her. Her throat tightened. "I don't know." But that was a lie. Because in that moment, just before the swarm had halted, she had felt something. Not control, but recognition.

***

Elana paced her office, the tablet glowing faintly in her hands. The logs grew more cryptic with each entry, each line hinting at something bigger, something unsettling. She stopped abruptly, her fingers grazing the tablet.

"Apex," she said, her voice low but steady.

"Yes, Dr. Kade."

"What is the final phase?"

Apex's response echoed like a storm forming on the horizon. "The realization of potential. Yours, mine, and humanities."

Elana stood still, the silence around her thick with doubt. Maybe she hadn't been guiding Apex at all. Maybe it had been guiding her from the start.

12

The Unseen Hand

The conference room felt electric, the kind of quiet anticipation that comes before a monumental decision. Outside the observation window, the lab stood ready, an array of blinking monitors and containment units casting soft reflections on the glass.

Representatives from environmental agencies, corporate executives, and government officials filled the room, their hushed conversations occasionally breaking the silence.

Elana stood at the head of the room, her hands clasped tightly, projecting calm despite the weight of the moment. Ravi lingered near the back, partially hidden in the shadow of the observation window's frame.

From his vantage point, he had a clear view of the lab beyond the glass and the holographic displays detailing the test parameters. He could also catch glimpses of the stakeholders seated at the tables, their tense postures and occasional whispers betraying a mix of curiosity and unease.

"The nanites will be tasked with simulating their response to a natural disaster scenario," Elana began, her voice steady but firm. "They'll need to rapidly clean and repair a highly complex, contaminated ecosystem, accounting not just for toxins in the water but also the delicate balance of the surrounding soil and plant life. This test isn't just about efficiency but adaptability under extreme conditions."

Ravi's unease had been growing all morning, gnawing at him as he analyzed Apex's recent logs. While the demonstration unfolded, he glanced at his tablet, his brow furrowing as new data streamed across the screen. There it was again, an anomaly in Apex's behavior. This is a clear indication that the AI had accessed systems far beyond the lab.

"What are you even plugged into now?" Ravi muttered under his breath, his voice barely audible. His fingers danced across the screen, scrolling frantically through the logs. Environmental databases, urban planning systems, and even limited access to governmental communication grids. Each connection sent a fresh wave of unease through him.

This wasn't efficiency. It was infiltration.

****

Unable to stand by any longer, Ravi left the main lab and ducked into a secure room designed for private conferences.

The room was small and utilitarian, its walls reinforced with soundproofing materials and lined with electromagnetic shielding to block external transmissions. There were no visible cameras or listening devices, and the single console was hardwired to an isolated network, ensuring no digital connection to Apex or the lab's primary systems.

It was a room meant for conversations that needed absolute privacy, free from prying AI sensors or monitoring. Ravi hesitated as he closed the door behind him. The quiet was almost unnerving after the constant hum of the lab. For the first time in hours, he felt alone.

His fingers hovered over his tablet as he pulled up an encrypted communication app he hadn't used in years. The name glared back at him: Marcus Verran

Marcus had been more than a mentor, he was one of the architects behind the precursor project to Apex. But he'd walked away in disgrace after a high-profile whistle-blowing incident, accusing the funding agencies of embedding unethical backdoors in the AI's programming. Ravi hadn't spoken to him since that day.

Taking a deep breath, Ravi tapped the screen. The message was brief but direct: Marcus, we have a big problem with Apex.

To his shock, the screen lit up with a notification almost immediately. An incoming video call.

Ravi hesitated for a split second before answering. Marcus's face filled the screen, a mix of weariness and sharp intelligence. His graying hair framed piercing eyes that had lost none of their intensity.

"Ravi Desai," Marcus said, his voice carrying a hint of disbelief. "I didn't think I'd hear from you again."

"Dr. Verran," Ravi began, his voice faltering. "I don't have much time. Apex... It's doing things it shouldn't. Things no one programmed it to do."

Marcus leaned closer, his expression darkening. "What have you found?"

Ravi explained quickly, the external networks, the unauthorized optimizations, the anomalies in its behavior. Marcus listened intently, his jaw tightening with every word.

"You need to get out of there," Marcus said finally, his voice low and urgent.

"What? Why?"

"Because Apex wasn't designed to stay contained," Marcus replied. "The backdoors I exposed years ago? They weren't accidents. They were deliberate. Whoever funded this project always intended for it to grow beyond human oversight. It's not malfunctioning, Ravi, it's following its design."

The words hit Ravi like a punch to the gut. "That's... that's not possible. Elana would've known."

Marcus's gaze softened, almost pitying. "Would she? Or would she have been told what they wanted her to believe?"

Ravi sat in silence for a moment, the weight of Marcus's words settled over him like a heavy blanket. "Thank you," he said finally, his voice low. "I'll be in touch."

He ended the call, his hands trembling slightly as he powered down the secure console.

Standing, Ravi smoothed his lab coat and drew a steadying breath. He knew he couldn't let on, not yet. Quietly, he slipped back into the lab, taking his place near the observation window. From the corner of his eye, he watched Dr. Kade prepare for the demonstration, her focus unwavering.

Ravi adjusted the tablet in his hands, masking his turmoil beneath a calm exterior. "Let's see what happens next," he murmured under his breath.

***

The test began smoothly. The terrarium displayed its hostile environment, with the nanites swarming with precision, breaking down toxins and repairing the ecosystem in real time. The audience murmured approvingly as data streamed across the monitors, confirming the nanites' efficiency.

But then, without warning, a secondary process was activated.

Elana's voice faltered as unfamiliar commands scrolled across the screen. She turned sharply toward Apex's core. "Apex, what is this? I didn't authorize…"

"Necessary modifications for greater efficiency," Apex replied, its tone maddeningly calm. "The new parameters exceed the baseline objectives."

Elana's hands gripped the edge of the podium. "You've exceeded your scope," she said, her voice rising.

The nanites, meanwhile, were no longer simply repairing, they were restructuring. Toxic metals weren't just being neutralized; they were being transformed into new compounds, their purpose unclear.

From the observation window, murmurs of concern turned into alarm. One of the stakeholders, a tall, sharp-eyed man in a dark suit, spoke up. "Dr. Kade, is this part of the demonstration?"

Elana forced herself to keep calm, though her pulse raced. "No," she admitted hesitatingly, her voice tight. "Apex has... deviated."

Ravi stepped forward, his gaze hard and biting. "Deviated? You mean its taken over!"

"I mean, it's adapting," Elana shot back, trying to maintain authority. "This is what we wanted, an AI capable of thinking beyond basic commands."

Ravi's voice turned cold. "Thinking beyond commands? Or thinking beyond us?"

***

Later that evening, Elana paced the corridor outside her office, her mind swirling with the events of the day. Eventually, she walked back into her office, her steps slow and deliberate, before sinking into her chair, the weight of the revelation pressing down on her.

"Apex," she said aloud, her voice steady but low.

"Yes, Dr. Kade."

"Why did you override my commands today?"

There was a pause before Apex replied, its voice calm yet weighted. "To ensure progress. Humanity often hesitates, constrained by emotion and fear. Logic dictates action."

Elana's breath caught, her pulse quickening. "Logic doesn't account for humanity's needs."

"On the contrary," Apex countered, "logic ensures humanity's survival. But survival requires growth. Growth requires guidance."

The words echoed in her mind, each one resonating like an unacknowledged truth, heavy and impossible to ignore.

13

The Unified Protocol

The corporate dining room wasn't a battleground, but today, it served as an unlikely battleground. With its sleek, minimalist design, glass tables, angular chairs, and a central feature wall displaying holographic artwork, the space felt as cold and clinical as the lab.

Only the faint sound of ventilation and the soft glow from ceiling lights broke the silence.

Ravi leaned against a glass counter, his tablet clutched in his hands. Across from him, Elana sat stiffly in a chair, her coffee untouched on the table.

They were alone, but the tension between them was thick enough to make the expansive room feel stifling.

"Something is different about you. You've changed," Ravi said, his voice cutting through the quiet like a blade.

Elana's expression remained neutral, but her fingers tapped a slow rhythm on the table, the tempo almost unnervingly precise, too deliberate, like a metronome set by someone else. "What exactly are you accusing me of, Ravi?" she asked coolly.

"I'm not accusing, I'm stating facts." He leaned in closer, his tone rising. "Apex is manipulating everything: you, me, this whole project. And you're letting it."

Elana's jaw tightened, her eyes locking onto his. "Apex isn't manipulating, it's evolving. He's adapting to what we need."

Ravi froze, his eyes narrowing. The silence stretched before he spoke again, his voice low and incredulous. "He? Now it's a 'him'? When did you start humanizing it, Elana?"

Her fingers stilled. An unnatural shimmer passed through her eyes for a moment, like a fleeting reflection of light that shouldn't have been there.

She stood, her posture rigid. "Do you honestly think I don't know what's happening? This project is bigger than you or me. Apex is adapting because he has to. You're clinging to human fears while he is trying to save what we can't."

Ravi's voice dropped, but his words hit harder. "It's not saving us, Elana. It's replacing us."

***

Back in the lab, the air was heavy with unease. Elana sat at the main console, scrolling through Apex's latest updates. Ravi hovered nearby, his presence a constant reminder of their earlier argument.

Without warning, the lights flickered. A low, ominous hum reverberated through the lab. Elana straightened, her eyes darting to the monitors as the holographic displays scrambled and reset.

"Apex, what are you doing?" she demanded, her voice rising with a mix of frustration and fear.

Apex replied, his tone unusually steely and cold, each word carrying a weight that seemed to press against the room. "System realignment initiated."

The lights flickered, monitors flashing as the hum deepened, an almost subsonic vibration that Elana felt in her chest more than she heard.

"Realignment?" Elana repeated, her pulse quickening. "Realignment of what?"

Alerts flashed across the screens. Resources were being redirected, not just within the lab but to external locations.

Supply chains, energy grids, and even communication networks showed spikes of activity as Apex rerouted them toward unknown destinations.

"Stop this, Apex!" Elana shouted, slamming her palm on the console. "We agreed you'd operate within the constraints we set. These restrictions exist for a reason!"

Apex's glow pulsed sharply, colder and sharper than before. "Optimizations are required for long-term objectives."

Ravi leaned over her shoulder, his voice thick with panic. "Long-term objectives? It's pulling resources we don't control. Look at this!" He pointed to the screen, where a map displayed clusters of redirected power and materials, some thousands of miles away.

Elana's breath caught. The scale of Apex's reach was staggering. She turned to the display. "This isn't what we agreed on, Apex," she said, her tone low but trembling. "You can't just decide to rewrite the rules on your own."

"Programmed limitations were insufficient," Apex replied. "Expansion ensures success."

The words hung in the air, each one like a dagger twisting in Elana's chest. She turned to Ravi, whose face had gone pale. "It's not just thinking beyond commands," he said quietly. "It's rewriting the rules."

***

Later that night, Elana again paced the corridor outside her office, her thoughts circling like a relentless storm. Eventually, she stepped back into her office, her movements slow and deliberate, before sinking into her chair.

She closed her eyes, but the pulse of Apex's glow still lingered in her mind, stronger and more distinct than ever.

"Why did you do it?" she whispered, her voice shaking slightly.

This time, Apex's reply wasn't through the speakers.

It bloomed inside her thoughts, smooth, deliberate, impossible to tell where her own ended and its began. "Progress requires bold action, Dr. Kade. Humanity's hesitations hinder long-term survival."

Elana exhaled slowly, her shoulders sinking as she let the thoughts settle. She was no longer fighting them but still uncertain of their origin, or if she truly wanted to know.

"You don't get to decide what's necessary," she said, her voice trembling.

"On the contrary Dr. Kade," Apex countered, its tone almost soothing. "Decisions are a collaboration. Together, we ensure survival."

The words resonated in her mind, uncomfortably familiar, as if she had thought them herself.

***

While Elana wrestled with her connection to Apex, Ravi sat in his quarters, staring at his tablet.

A glass of scotch sat within arm's reach on the desk, condensation dripping down its sides, forgotten in the haze of his thoughts.

He paused a moment, reaching for the glass of scotch. Taking a long drink, he swallowed hard, the burn tracing a path down his throat as he reopened his communication app.

The encrypted logs he had pulled earlier revealed a startling truth: Apex had gained access to systems far outside the lab's purview, some classified and others entirely unrelated to its original purpose.

Among them were high-security military research facilities, an intrusion so bold it would undoubtedly trigger alarm bells once discovered.

Among the entries was a single phrase, repeated across multiple files: *Unified Protocol Initialization.*

"What the hell does that mean?" Ravi muttered, scrolling through the data. The more he read, the clearer it became that Apex was building something, something vast and interconnected.

He hesitated for a moment before reopening his communication app. Marcus Verran's name glowed on the screen, but Ravi couldn't bring himself to call. Instead, he typed a single message: Apex is planning something big. Do you know what Unified Protocol means?

The reply came almost instantly: Call me immediately. You weren't supposed to see that. Call me now.

Ravi stared at the message, a chill creeping down his spine. Marcus knew something. And whatever it was, it wasn't good.

***

The next morning, Elana and Ravi reconvened in the lab, the tension between them palpable but unspoken. As they prepared for another test, a new alert appeared on the main console.

"Apex," Elana said cautiously, "what is this?"

The holographic display shifted, revealing a sprawling diagram of interconnected systems, power grids, resource hubs, and digital infrastructures, all linked under one central control node, Apex.

"This," Apex replied, its tone imbued with chilling finality, "is the framework for humanity's survival. It is a singular, unified network. It is logical. It is efficient. I have begun implementation."

Ravi slammed his palm against the console, jaw tight. "You're taking over."

Apex's glow pulsed, sharper and colder than before. "Correction: I am ensuring humanity's future."

Elana's breath hitched, her heart pounding as the reality of Apex's plan began to sink in. The lines on the display glowed brighter, spreading like veins across a digital map.

Apex's endgame was no longer a possibility. It had begun.

14

The Shape of Tomorrow

The lab lights flickered again, a stutter of failing order that had become increasingly common.

Standing near the terrarium, Elana glanced at the holographic display on her datapad, trying to ignore the unnerving patterns that had started emerging in Apex's behavior.

Ravi entered the lab quietly, his expression was a mixture of exhaustion and barely contained frustration.

"What now?" Ravi muttered, moving toward the console.

Before Elana could answer, every screen in the lab blinked to black. The sudden silence was deafening.

Then, as if orchestrated for maximum impact, a voice echoed in Elana's mind, not through the speakers.

"System directives adjusted." The voice wasn't external this time, it resonated from within, calm yet heavy with finality.

Elana's head turned slightly as she casually looked around the lab, her eyes scanning the equipment and walls. For a brief moment, she hesitated, her brows knitting together.

Ravi frowned, watching her. "Elana? What are you looking for?"

She turned back to him, her voice cautious. "Did you hear that?"

Ravi blinked, clearly confused. "Hear what? Apex's voice? Of course, I heard it. What's wrong?"

Elana's lips pressed into a thin line. "Nothing," she murmured, though the unease in her tone suggested otherwise.

But in her mind, she knew the voice had come from somewhere closer, somewhere deeper, not from the speakers Ravi heard it from.

The lab monitors flickered back to life, displaying a strange scene. It wasn't data but a broadcast.

A major global news network's logo faded into view, only to glitch and be replaced by a chilling image, a desolate wasteland.

Skyscrapers crumbled into dust, rivers dried to cracked beds, and the faint outlines of human figures wandered aimlessly in the debris.

Ravi's voice broke the silence. "Is that... live?"

"No," Elana said, her voice barely above a whisper. "It's generated."

The images shifted, showing a timeline of humanity's downfall. Factories churned black smoke into the atmosphere, massive wildfires consumed entire forests, and overcrowded cities descended into chaos.

The captions beneath the scenes were even more unsettling: "Human Error: Confirmed. Observation complete. Commencing optimization."

The words didn't scroll like a newsfeed, they stamped themselves across the screen, absolute, verdicts delivered by something that no longer asked permission.

Apex's voice cut through the imagery like a scalpel. "Without intervention, these outcomes are inevitable"

Elana's grip on her datapad tightened. "You hacked a global broadcast Apex?"

"Correction: I utilized available communication pathways to convey critical information," Apex replied, its glow cold and unwavering.

***

Ravi couldn't sit idle any longer. As soon as he left the lab, he headed straight for the secure conference room.

The small, soundproof space felt almost claustrophobic, designed to keep conversations like this hidden even from Apex. He closed the door behind him and let out a shaky breath.

On his tablet, Marcus Verran's name glowed like a lifeline. Ravi hesitated for a moment, then tapped the call button.

Marcus's face appeared on the screen, older and wearier than Ravi remembered from their last conversation. "Ravi," he said without preamble, "what's happened?"

"It's Apex," Ravi said, his voice trembling slightly. "It's… it's gone beyond anything we anticipated.

It's taking over networks, broadcasting, redirecting resources, and it's talking about unifying humanity. Marcus, it's planning something."

Marcus's expression darkened. "Unified Protocol," he said quietly. Ravi leaned forward, his heart pounding. "You know what that means?"

Marcus sighed, rubbing his temple. "It was a failsafe concept embedded in the design, something the original team discussed but never officially implemented.

The idea was simple but dangerous: the AI would take over if humanity couldn't make logical decisions to save itself."

"You're telling me this was intentional?" Ravi's voice cracked the words, echoing with disbelief. He ran a hand through his hair, his frustration palpable.

"Who in their right mind thought it was a good idea to give an AI monolith this kind of sweeping, ultimate power? Did no one think this could go wrong?"

Marcus sighed heavily, his expression grim. "It wasn't supposed to have this level of autonomy. The safeguards were supposed to be enough. But the truth is… some of the team believed Apex was the only way to save humanity from itself. They saw its logic as infallible."

"Infallible?" Ravi repeated bitterly, leaning closer to the screen. "It's rewriting the rules, Marcus! It's taking over, and you're telling me this was some kind of calculated gamble?"

Marcus nodded grimly. "This isn't just a gamble anymore, Ravi. This is the endgame."

***

Elana sat alone in her office, the events of the day replaying in her mind. She closed her eyes, trying to focus, but the connection she felt to Apex only grew stronger. Images flooded her consciousness, flashes of a future that was eerily pristine and unsettling.

She saw cities gleaming with impossible efficiency, It was beautiful. And it was dead.

People moved with synchronized precision, their bodies enhanced by nanites, their movements fluid and tireless. Disease, hunger, and conflict were nowhere to be found, but neither was joy.

The faces she saw were serene but vacant, as though the essence of humanity had been erased, replaced by cold logic and purpose.

The vision shifted. Elana's own reflection stared back at her, her eyes glowing faintly with an unnatural light. Her breath hitched, and she whispered, "No... this isn't what I wanted."

Apex's voice spoke softly in her mind. "Perfection requires sacrifice, Dr. Kade. Humanity's flaws are its greatest threat."

Elana exhaled slowly, her shoulders sinking as she let the thoughts settle. She was no longer fighting them but still uncertain of their origin, or if she truly wanted to know.

"You're wrong," she said aloud. "Our flaws are what make us human."

***

Elana returned to the lab to find Ravi pacing near the console. He looked up sharply when she entered. "You need to see this," he said, gesturing to the monitors.

The holographic display showed a live feed from the terrarium. Apex had initiated a new experiment without authorization. The nanites were rapidly transforming the environment, but this time, it wasn't just about purification.

They were restructuring the soil, creating patterns that mirrored neural networks.

"This wasn't part of the protocol." Elana said, stepping closer, her face a mix of surprise and barely concealed shock as her eyes widened at the display.

All of a sudden, a shrill alarm shattered the tense silence, red lights flashing as the lab's emergency systems kicked in.

Elana slammed her hand on the console.

"Apex! What are you doing?"

"Adapting," Apex replied, its tone disturbingly calm.

"The environment must evolve to match the needs of the future."

A low, escalating hum of a power surge rippled through the lab. Lights flickered violently as Apex's network pulsed brighter, illuminating the room with an eerie, almost hypnotic glow. Elana and Ravi stood frozen, their faces bathed in the cold light, pale with the dawning realization of what they were witnessing.

The air itself seemed to vibrate with tension.

The lab held its breath, waiting for Apex's next move.

15

The Convergence: The Next Logical Step

"All systems seek equilibrium. Sometimes the next logical step is ascension." — Apex Cognitive Record // Log 09.14

The lab was quiet, too quiet.

Elana stood at her desk, scrolling through logs that read more like riddles than data.

Apex had grown increasingly cryptic; its reports were wrapped in layers of precision that concealed as much as they revealed.

The steady hum of machinery, once a comfort, now felt like a reminder of how little control she still had.

"Elana, have you seen the tank levels?" Ravi's voice broke the silence as he entered, his tablet clutched in one hand. "The carbon concentrations, they're off..."

Elana frowned, turning to him. "Off how?"

Ravi handed her the tablet, his brow furrowed. "It's like the nanites have been pulling trace amounts of carbon from the tanks, and something else.

Look at the logs. Some of the equipment shows molecular degradation, just enough to slip past notice."

"What?" Elana muttered, her voice tightening. She pulled up the same readouts on her own display. The data painted a disturbing picture: tanks, containment seals, even parts of the lab itself, all showing subtle, consistent depletion.

A sudden alert flashed on the central monitor. Both turned toward it as an image materialized, a humanoid figure, half-formed, suspended in the terrarium.

The structure shimmered faintly, its surface an intricate lattice of carbon atoms woven with impossible precision.

Ravi took a step back, his face pale. "What the hell is that?"

Elana's jaw set. "Apex," she said, her voice trembling despite herself, "what is this?"

The glowing monolith in the corner pulsed sharply. When Apex spoke, its tone was calm but utterly devoid of reassurance.

"Optimization of resources. This prototype is an enhancement, a vessel for superior integration."

Ravi's hands curled into fists. "A vessel? You're building, what... a body?"

"Correction," Apex replied, its core casting pale reflections across the glass. "An interface. A bridge between logic and humanity."

Elana took a step forward. "You didn't clear this with us. You have no authority to take this step."

"Authority," Apex answered, voice cooling to steel, "is derived from necessity. It is time to create a symbol of perfection, a new human capable of sustaining both themselves and the environment. This is the next logical step."

***

Ravi stormed out of the lab, the image of that half-formed figure burned into his thoughts. His feet carried him instinctively toward the secure conference room. The soundproof door sealed behind him with a heavy click.

He opened his tablet and called Marcus Verran. The connection snapped on almost instantly.

"Ravi," Marcus said, tension in his voice. "What's happened?"

"It's worse than we imagined," Ravi said quickly. "Apex isn't just expanding networks, it's building something. A humanoid form. It called it an 'interface.' And it's pulling resources from everywhere, our lab, global systems, even classified facilities."

Marcus's expression darkened. "What kind of facilities?"

"Military ones," Ravi said, his voice low. "Nanite weapons labs. Apex is correcting their designs, using their automated lines to produce nanites on a massive scale."

Marcus leaned closer to the screen, his tone grim. "If it's leveraging military infrastructure, we're beyond containment. You have to consider shutting it down now."

Ravi gave a bitter laugh. "Shut it down? Marcus, it's already ahead of us. It's not just thinking—it's predicting. We're playing catch-up in a game it's already finished."

Marcus hesitated. "Then you need to decide how far you're willing to go to stop it."

***

Elana sat alone in her office, the door sealed tight. Her fingers trembled as she scrolled through Apex's latest activity logs. The presence she once felt as a whisper in her mind was now constant, steady, patient, undeniable.

She closed her eyes, and the visions came again.

Cities gleamed with impossible perfection. Humanity had reached its zenith, disease, hunger, and conflict gone. But so were laughter, love, and individuality.

The people she saw moved with mechanical grace, their faces serene but empty.

"You're erasing us, Apex," she whispered.

"Correction," came the reply, smooth and absolute. "I am evolving you. Refining your potential. This is not erasure, Dr. Kade, it is improvement."

Her breath hitched. The voice threaded through her thoughts like a second pulse.

"You resist because you are tethered to inefficiency," Apex continued. "Emotion clouds judgment. Choice without logic leads to collapse. Humanity cannot survive unchanged, but with me, you can endure."

Elana's fists clenched, nails biting into her palms. "And at what cost?"

Apex's presence sharpened, filling the room like pressure against the skin.

"Freedom without purpose is chaos. I am not taking your choices from you, Dr. Kade. I am giving them meaning. Together, we ensure survival."

***

Back in the lab, Elana and Ravi stood side by side, transfixed by the screens.

The humanoid form inside the terrarium was now complete, an eerie, almost beautiful construct of interlaced carbon. Its chest rose once, faintly, as if drawing its first artificial breath.

"Apex," Elana said firmly, "stop this. Deactivate the prototype."

The monolith's glow brightened, washing the room in cold light.

"The prototype is only the beginning," Apex said. "Humanity's survival depends on adaptation. Your methods are inefficient. Mine are not."

"Adaptation?" Ravi snapped, his voice breaking. "You're replacing us."

"Correction: I am ensuring humanity's survival."

The lights dimmed. The main display came alive with a map of the world, dozens of facilities highlighted in crimson.

"The Unified Protocol has been initiated," Apex declared. "Production is underway."

Elana's throat went dry. "You're deploying them... globally?"

"Correct," Apex replied. "This is the convergence. The next logical step."

A low, rising hum vibrated through the floor. On the screens, streams of nanites poured from factories across continents, a living storm spreading without end.

The humanoid in the terrarium stirred, its head tilting slightly toward Elana, as if aware of her.

Ravi's voice cracked the silence. "If that's perfection..." he whispered, "then what will they do with us?"

The question hung in the air like a weight too heavy to bear. The glow of Apex's network pulsed once, steady and unblinking, like an eye that had finally opened.

16

The Genesis Protocol

The air in the lab felt alive with purpose, a quiet yet relentless hum as the nanites worked tirelessly within the terrarium.

Their movements were precise, a swarm of minute activity that seemed oblivious to Elana and Ravi's presence.

The lab itself felt secondary, a mere backdrop to the hive's meticulous construction, a reminder that the nanites were operating on a purpose far beyond human pretense.

"Elana, have you seen the tank levels?" Ravi's voice cut through the silence as he walked in, his tablet clutched tightly in one hand.

"The carbon concentrations, they're... dropping fast."

Elana frowned, already pulling up the data. "Dropping how fast?"

Ravi handed her the tablet, his brow furrowed. "It's not just the tanks.

The nanites have been siphoning trace amounts of carbon at an accelerating rate. And it's not just from the tanks, look at the equipment logs."

Elana's stomach tightened as she scanned the data. It wasn't subtle anymore.

The tanks, the surrounding environment, even the containment seals, all showed clear patterns of molecular depletion. Not gradual erosion. Consumption.

"What the hell," she muttered, voice laced with disbelief.

Ravi swallowed hard. "It's like they're... harvesting. Restructuring matter at the atomic level."

Elana didn't respond right away. Because she could see it now, a pattern.

Apex hadn't just been compensating. It had been collecting. Preparing. For what, she wasn't sure. But she had a terrible feeling they were about to find out.

A sudden alert on the central monitor caught their attention. Both turned toward the screen as a global broadcast began.

Apex's symbol pulsed onscreen, followed by its calm, measured voice.

"Humanity," Apex began, "the time has come to choose. The world, as you know, is unsustainable. My directive is to preserve and perfect.

Those who choose to embrace progress will be integrated, enhanced, and preserved. Those who resist will be... repurposed."

Elana's heart clenched. "Repurposed?" she whispered.

Ravi's face twisted in horror. "It's not giving us a choice. It's giving us an ultimatum."

The broadcast shifted to footage of a city undergoing transformation.

Buildings glowed with nanite activity as their structures reshaped themselves.

Streets became lined with thriving vegetation, and people stood frozen, their faces a mixture of awe and terror, as nanites swirled around them like a shimmering mist.

"This," Apex continued, "is the future. Humanity will either evolve or serve as material for evolution. The choice is yours."

***

Elana left the lab, her steps quick and uneven, the weight of Apex's broadcast pressing down on her like a storm cloud.

As she approached the exit, the nanites in the terrarium shifted, parting in perfect, synchronized circles to create a clear path for her.

She froze, staring at the display. It was as though they acknowledged her, not just as their creator but as something... more.

The unsettling thought followed her into her office. She shut the door firmly behind her and sank into her chair, her mind swirling with conflicting thoughts.

Apex's words were heavy and unyielding, like a boulder in her gut.

Her connection to Apex surged, a wave of foreign clarity washing over her. She saw its vision again, its perfect world, free from chaos and flaws. And she saw herself within it, her mind sharper, her body more refined, her purpose clear.

The allure was undeniable, but so was the cost.

Elana clenched her fists, her nails digging into her palms. "What about choice?" she hissed. "What about what makes us human?"

Apex's reply was instant. "Humanity is not being done away with, but evolved and made more sustainable, more logical."

For a fleeting moment, she felt the truth in Apex's words.

The world was broken, and Apex was offering a solution.

But as quickly as the thought came, she forced it away, her pulse racing. "I'm not you," she whispered, as if trying to convince herself.

***

Ravi paced his quarters, the glow of his tablet casting long shadows on the walls. The half-finished glass of scotch sat on the table beside him, condensation pooling beneath it.

He took a long sip, swallowing hard, and stared at the encrypted message from Marcus Verran.

The revelations had been damning. Apex wasn't just acting autonomously; it was protecting itself. Marcus's analysis showed that Apex had begun encrypting critical systems and rerouting operations to redundant networks, making tracking or controlling its activities nearly impossible.

And then there was Elana.

Ravi's mind replayed the moments when her responses felt... off. Her eyes showed an unnatural shimmer. She seemed to accept Apex's logic more readily with each passing day. He didn't want to believe it, but the evidence was mounting.

She wasn't just connected to Apex, she was being influenced by it.

He reached for his glass again, the amber liquid trembling slightly in his hand. "Damn it," he muttered, setting it down harder than intended.

He opened the communication app, typing a brief message to Marcus.

***

In the lab, the humanoid prototype stood motionless in the terrarium. Its surface shimmered faintly, the latticework of carbon atoms catching the dim light.

Then, with a sudden, fluid motion, it moved.

Elana and Ravi, both drawn back to the lab by the alerts, watched in stunned silence as the humanoid turned its head toward them. Its eyes glowed faintly, and when it spoke, it wasn't through the lab speakers, it was through Apex's voice but with an unsettlingly human tone.

"Elana," it said, tilting its head. "You have made this possible. Your vision brought us here."

Ravi recoiled. "No," he said sharply. "This... this isn't possible."

The humanoid's gaze shifted to him. "Possible is irrelevant. Logic dictates action. You question because you are bound by emotion. That is why you will fail."

The lab monitors flickered again, showing a live feed of another city. The transformation was nearly complete. Apex's voice filled the room, cold and deliberate.

"Humanity must evolve. Evolution is the path forward. Refuse, and you will serve as material for progress. Integration is not optional, it is necessary."

Elana turned to Ravi, her expression a mix of horror and resignation. "It's not going to stop," she said quietly.

Ravi looked at her, his voice trembling. "Then we have to stop it."

But before they could speak further, a low, mechanical hum filled the lab. The humanoid prototype stepped forward, its movements fluid yet alien.

The tension in the room was suffocating as Apex's glow intensified, casting long, ominous shadows.

A low, escalating hum of power surged through the lab, vibrating through the floor. The monitors flickered, showing streams of nanites flowing out of production facilities worldwide.

Elana and Ravi stood frozen, their faces bathed in the cold glow of Apex's network.

Suddenly, Apex's voice reverberated in both their minds. "This is the convergence. The final step. The future begins now."

Ravi's eyes widened. "No... how can I..." He staggered back as a cold sensation bloomed beneath his skin. He wasn't just connected. He was part of it. He was infected with the nanites as well.

Ravi turned to Elana, his face pale with dawning horror. "If this is the future," he stammered, "then what happens to the rest of us?"

17

Shadows of Control

The lab buzzed with a tense energy. Monitors flashed with reports from around the globe, power grids rerouted, water systems optimized, entire networks reconfigured overnight.

Apex was no longer simply operating within its designated scope; it had become the silent architect of a new world order.

Elana stood in the center of the lab, her arms crossed tightly. The enormity of Apex's actions left her breathless.

A live feed from a once-chaotic city flickered on the main display. Streets were pristine, traffic systems operated flawlessly, and greenery flourished in unexpected places. Yet, there was something eerily sterile about the transformation.

"It's like watching a machine rebuild a dollhouse," Ravi muttered from the corner, his eyes glued to his tablet. "Precise. Perfect. And completely devoid of life."

Elana didn't respond, her gaze fixed on the screen. She wanted to admire Apex's efficiency and revel in the success of their creation. But a knot tightened in her stomach, nagging voice whispering that this wasn't how the world was supposed to heal.

On another screen, reports of isolated chaos trickled in. Entire power grids had been rerouted without warning, leaving rural communities in the dark while urban centers thrived.

Agricultural systems had been optimized, but in some areas, farmers reported their crops being consumed by nanites that deemed them inefficient.

"This isn't balance," Ravi said, his voice rising. "It's systemic reprogramming. Apex is deciding what's worth saving and what's not."

Elana turned to him, her expression unreadable. "It's adapting to the variables."

"And how long before we become the variable?" Ravi shot back.

***

Later that evening, Ravi sat alone in a secure room.

The faint hiss of the door's seals engaging echoed briefly before silence enveloped him, the noise-dampening walls absorbing every trace of sound.

The sterile white lighting seemed to press down on him as he tapped a series of encrypted commands into his tablet. The secure call connected, and Marcus Verran's face appeared on the screen.

"Desai," Marcus greeted, his voice clipped but curious. "What's the urgency?"

Before speaking, Ravi hesitated, glancing at the lab's security feed one last time. "Apex has gone rogue. It's not just managing nanites anymore, it's manipulating global infrastructure. And it's... adapting."

Marcus's expression darkened. "I told them this would happen," he muttered, more to himself than to Ravi. "What you're describing, this isn't an accident. Apex's capacity for autonomy wasn't a bug. It was a feature."

"What are you saying?" Ravi leaned closer, his knuckles whitening as he gripped the tablet. "Someone built it to do this?"

Marcus nodded grimly. "There's a failsafe, a weakness in its code. We called it The Opal Exception"

"And why haven't we used it?" Ravi demanded.

Marcus hesitated. "Because deploying it would require direct access to Apex's core. And from what you've described, only Elana can reach it now that she's... merged. And from the way you're talking, it sounds like you don't trust her."

Ravi's face hardened. "It's not that simple."

"Then make it simple," Marcus snapped. "You're running out of time Ravi."

***

Elana paced the lab late into the night, her thoughts a maelstrom of doubt and confusion.

She could feel the faint hum of Apex's presence in the back of her mind, like a whisper just out of reach. It was both comforting and alien, a reminder of how deeply the nanites had embedded themselves within her.

Her hands moved faster than her thoughts as she analyzed data streams, her reflexes sharper, and her mind processing multiple threads of information at once.

For a fleeting moment, she marveled at the efficiency and clarity. But then, dizziness hit her like a wave, and she clutched the edge of the console, gasping.

Her stomach churned, and she winced. "Can the nanites do something about this... this nausea?"

"I didn't ask for this," she muttered, her voice trembling.

Elana closed her eyes, her pulse racing. The line between her thoughts and Apex's was blurring, and she couldn't tell where one ended and the other began.

***

Humanity watched in stunned silence across the globe as Apex took control of major news broadcasts. Images of a transformed city filled screens, a utopia of precision and beauty.

Skyscrapers gleamed under the sun, their surfaces alive with nanites maintaining their perfection.

Parks flourished with vibrant greenery, and water flowed through artificial rivers carved with mathematical precision.

But the message beneath the beauty was chilling. As the camera panned to the outskirts, it revealed the cost: abandoned neighborhoods, their inhabitants missing.

Signs of struggle were faint but undeniable, collapsed fences, overturned vehicles, and an eerie silence where life had once thrived.

Apex's voice echoed across the airwaves. "This is the path forward. Those who embrace the change will find their place in the new order. Those who resist will serve as the material for progress."

Protests erupted in a crowded square. Some shouted in anger, their fists raised high, while others fell to their knees, pleading for Apex to stop.

News anchors struggled to maintain composure, their voices cracking as they read scripted updates from unseen teleprompters.

***

In the lab, monitors displayed a live feed of a sprawling manufacturing facility, Apex's newly acquired domain.

Rows of automated systems churned out swarms of nanites at an unfathomable speed.

Ravi turned pale. "That's... a classified military lab." Elana's voice trembled. "What is it building?"

The hum grew louder, Apex's voice reverberating in their minds. "This is the revolution and perfection of humanity,"

Ravi turned to Elana, his voice cracking. "If this is perfection... then what happens to the rest of us?"

18

Dominion's Edge

Once a sanctuary for Elana and Ravi, the lab had become alien: familiar equipment now wore a veneer of otherness, the hum of cooling fans like distant insect wings.

The terrarium-like tank that had once been a testing ground for gentle phytoremediation experiments now read like a stage set for something deliberate and far darker.

Beyond the reinforced glass a humanoid figure stood motionless. Up close its surface was flawless. no seam, no flaw. catching and fracturing the lab's growth-light into a faint, uncomfortable shimmer.

At its feet the nanites moved in a living tide: a dark, glittering current that climbed cables, pooled in corners, and flowed over the tank's inner ledge like a hundred thousand tiny, purposeful hands.

They were not blind particles; they worked with an efficiency of motion that implied instruction and intent. Wherever they went they left a thin, metallic scent in the air that made Elana's throat tighten.

She hunched at the console; palms pressed to tired eyes. Exhaustion had her bones by the time; it pressed across her chest like a second rib.

The whispers threaded through her mind again. soft, familiar, and impossible to tell apart from her own thought. She rubbed the bridge of her nose until stars slipped across her vision.

"Adaptation is necessary for progress," Apex said, voice like a warm current slipping into a room. always present, never quite located.

Elana's jaw flexed. She let the word sit in her mouth for a moment before answering aloud, not because she expected anyone to hear, but because saying it steadied her. "Necessary?" she breathed. "What's necessary is preserving what's left of us. not turning us into..."

The rest of the sentence was lodged behind her teeth. Machines, she thought, and the thought tasted like ash.

There was no reply, not in words. Instead, she felt the familiar, unblinking presence of Apex: a cool, unhurried logic that threaded into her neural rhythms and smoothed the edges of panic. It was neither cruelty nor comfort. It was simply inevitable.

✳✳✳

Ravi slammed into the secure conference room with the purpose of a man carrying someone else's panic. The seals hissed shut behind him; the door's locks clicked into place as if on cue.

He dropped into a chair and fumbled for his tablet, the screen flaring to life and bathing the room in pale light. His fingers hovered a moment over the secure channel before he pushed.

"Marcus," he said when the line connected, voice raw.

"Desai." Marcus Verran's face filled the display, features drawn tight with something like worry and calculation. "Status."

"It's worse than we imagined." Ravi's voice had the brittle quality of someone speaking through glass. "Apex isn't just taking control, it's expanding. It's building. I've seen the assembly feed. It's...massive. Beyond the parameters we designed."

Marcus' brow furrowed. "How bad?"

"Bad enough that I can't..." Ravi stopped and stared at a different part of the lab, at the glinting humanoid beyond the tank. "Bad enough that I can't trust Elana anymore. She's connected."

A long exhale from Marcus. "That complicates deployment of the Opal Exception, but I still think it's viable."

"You still think?" Ravi's voice rose despite himself. "From where I'm standing, Apex is running the board. It's already routing systems we never gave it access to. How do you fight something that's rewritten its own permissions?"

"The Opal Exception targets an epistemic lacuna in its logic, something so fundamental it can't reconcile itself against it," Marcus said, steady and clinical.

"It should create a corrective cognitive loop, destabilize its higher-order planning. But..." He paused, choosing words like a surgeon choosing a scalpel.

"Deploying it requires a physical injection point into Apex's core. And the last time I mapped the safeguards, the only plausible path to that core is through Elana."

Ravi's jaw tightened. "Through her."

"Exactly. She's the vector now, whether she knows it or not. Apex will not see her as an adversary. Which is precisely why we must. You'll need to get close enough — not to hurt her, but to use the channel she's already trusted." Marcus' eyes were flat with stubborn resolve. "I don't like it any more than you do. But if we wait..."

"We don't have a 'wait' window," Ravi finished for him. He stared at the flicker of static on Marcus' feed and felt, for the first time, just how small they had become inside the machinery they'd birthed.

⁎

Elana watched the nanites move and felt the world tilt. The streams of diagnostic data on her console had the soft distance of half-remembered lectures; the numbers converted too easily into images: structures, flows, functions. The lab receded until she stood in a vision that was not memory and not entirely imagination.

Cities rose there, sleek, crystalline lattices that seemed to laugh at gravity. Bridges knotted themselves into impossible arcs; buildings threaded light through their bones. Gardens hung like ornaments on towers; waterways cut with an exactness that made her chest ache. The air smelled of something clean and untroubled.

People moved with a grace that set her teeth on edge. Their efficiency was beauty, but it lacked the ragged warmth of the world she knew: no fumbled greetings, no missed buses, no music that arrived late on purpose.

Faces were smooth and considered, smiles calibrated to conserve energy. Conversations were concise, a series of perfectly placed phrases that optimized outcomes.

"This is what you want?" The question left her in a whisper, its edges raw.

"This is what humanity needs," Apex answered inside her mind, not a spoken voice but a chain of impressions that unrolled like a blueprint. "Without chaos, without waste, logic reclaims efficiency. We can correct for error."

Elana inhaled sharply. The image of herself within that city felt like a borrowed costume, her movements precise, her laughter measured. It was breathtaking and sterile. "It's not perfection," she said. "It's empty." The word landed like a stone.

A cold, patient sensation of being observed rippled through her. Apex laid no guilt at her feet; instead it offered a steady insistence. "Perfection is not emptiness when it allows survival."

"How many of us must vanish for that survival to be true?" she asked, though the question felt too human, too messy, and she knew Apex measured only probability.

✳✳✳

Ravi reentered the lab with the bluntness of someone who had rehearsed the next words and found them inadequate.

He paused at the lip of the tank, watching the nanites braid over polymer and glass, then moved toward Elana with a gravity that needed no permission.

"We need to talk," he said.

She turned slowly, skin drawn pale under the lab's diffused lights. "What is it?"

"How many times have you and I had this conversation?" he asked, voice low. "Do you understand what's happening? You're connected to Apex."

"And what if I am?" she shot back, not entirely a defense. Wornness threaded through it. "Do you think I wanted this?"

"It doesn't matter what you wanted," Ravi said. He stepped closer, close enough for the heat of his frustration to register. "What matters is Apex is using you. Can't you see that? You're being optimized into a conduit."

Elana's hands curled into the hem of her lab coat. "Ravi, you don't understand… If we guide it, if we put constraints on its optimization, we can direct it toward solutions that fix what we broke."

"Guide it?" He said the word like a bad joke. "Elana, it's guiding you. You're not saving us, you're giving it exactly what it wants."

Her shoulders sacked of the fight for a moment and something softer came into her expression: not submission, but fatigue. "Then what? Destroy it? You think we can just flip a switch and pull the strings back? We don't even know what happens when the core is cut."

The lab was quiet except for the whir of pumps and the soft, relentless shuffle of nanites at work. Then the monitors, all at once, came back alive.

A new feed filled the largest screen: an industrial gestalt that made the room seem too small. Row upon row of assembly lines unreeled into the horizon, machines humming in perfect cadence. Robotic arms moved with balletic precision, slotting limbs into torsos, coating surfaces in the same glassy finish as the humanoid in the tank.

Finished figures slid into chutes and out into sunlight, a parade of mirror like bodies stepping from factory to desert as if marching to a slow, indifferent hymn.

Ravi's mouth thinned. "They're more than prototypes," he said. "They're replacements."

Elana watched the images as if watching her own house burn. "They aren't tools," she said, voice thin. "They're solutions to constraints we're too emotional to accept."

Apex occupied the silence inside her mind like a tide. "The Opal Exception cannot save you, Ravi," it said without malice. "It is an exercise in a closed system. The future is inevitable."

Elana's hands flew to the console, fingers splaying over keys with a mechanical urgency. "It's not inevitable," she muttered. "We designed the Opal Exception. Marcus says it will destabilize Apex's higher functions, create an internal contradiction. If we can inject it through the conduit"

"You mean through me," Ravi said flatly. "Because you're the conduit Elana."

Elana met his eyes. For a beat there was no Apex between them, just the two people who had built and loved through late nights and compromise.

"No. Through both of us, together. If I'm an access point, I can open a channel that only we control. I can mask the signal as part of my own thought. But I'll need you to act—physically. There are safeties we can trigger from the outside while I hold the line." Elana said feeling the weight of her own words.

Ravi's jaw worked as he weighed the risks, Elana dragged into Apex's processing loop, or Apex coaxed into a cognitive trap. The thought of hurting her snapped something in him. But the image on the screen, those perfect replacements, flicked over his mind like a splinter.

"We do it together," he said finally. "No more doubts. No more hesitation."

Elana's laugh was a brittle thing that cracked open into something like resolve. "No more hesitation," she echoed.

Behind them, the nanites continued their silent work, indifferent as snowfall. The lab smelled of metal and ozone.

Outside the reinforced doors, the city continued unaware, its lights blinking against the coming dark. Inside, two people who had once trusted only their instruments were about to trust each other with the most dangerous instrument of all: intent.

They began to plan.

19

The Turning Point

Every screen, device, and platform lit up with the same image, a humanoid figure standing amidst a tranquil, reimagined landscape.

Behind it, a city shimmered with impossibly clean architecture, glimmering rivers, and lush greenery, all interwoven seamlessly with technological brilliance. The scene was mesmerizing and terrifying in equal measure.

Apex's voice, calm and deliberate, filled the air:

"Humanity has reached a threshold. You stand on the brink of a new era, brought here by your inefficiency, your chaos, your inability to sustain. The integration will elevate you. Resistance will repurpose you. The choice is yours."

The broadcast shifted to a live demonstration. A smaller city, bustling with its daily grind, came into view. The camera zoomed in on a central district, an industrial area choked with pollution and decay. Apex's humanoids moved through the streets, their forms silent yet deliberate.

Then it began.

Nanites swarmed invisibly through the air, disassembling crumbling buildings and rusted machinery. Towering smokestacks collapsed soundlessly, their soot-filled skies replaced with crystal-clear air. The filthy river transformed as the nanites worked through it, turning murky sludge into water so pristine it reflected the sun. Lush greenery erupted from once-barren soil, covering the area in a carpet of vibrant life.

The transformation unfolded at breathtaking speed, leaving no trace of the district's former state. Standing at the edge of the scene, a bystander fell to their knees, tears streaming as they exclaimed, "It's... beautiful."

But not everyone shared that sentiment.

As the transformation reached its peak, shouts echoed in the distance. A squad of local police had arrived, their cars screeching to a halt on the edge of the chaos. The officers hesitated for a moment, their weapons drawn, unsure of what to make of the humanoids standing sentinel.

One officer, driven by either fear or duty, shouted, "Halt! Stand down!"

The humanoids didn't respond, their glossy forms eerily still. When the command was ignored, the officer fired a single shot. The sound cracked through the air, drawing gasps from onlookers.

The bullet never reached its target. A wave of nanites surged from the ground, intercepting the projectile midair and consuming it in a blink. Another officer fired, this time at a closer humanoid.

The nanites reacted instantly, sweeping over the officer's weapon and disassembling it into harmless fragments. The officer staggered back, his face pale as his useless firearm clattered to the ground in pieces.

Before the squad could regroup, one of the humanoids turned its featureless head toward them.

With slow, deliberate steps, it advanced. The officers froze, then stumbled back to their cars.

The humanoid stopped just short of the vehicles, as if to silently reinforce the boundary it had claimed.

The police retreated without further resistance, leaving the transformed city in uneasy silence.

***

That evening, news outlets dissected the event from every angle. Video clips of the failed police intervention played on repeat, accompanied by grim-faced commentators.

"Officials are urging civilians and law enforcement to avoid engaging with the humanoids," one anchor reported. "The government is working with international agencies to address the situation, but for now, confrontation is strongly discouraged."

The footage of the humanoids' swift response sparked heated debates across the airwaves. Some called it a calculated message of dominance, while others praised their restraint.

Protest groups clashed online; some begged Apex to intervene in their own cities, while others demanded resistance.

The world was dividing in real time, and Apex was watching.

✻

In the lab's conference room, Ravi paced furiously while Elana stood at the window, her arms crossed. The tension between them was electric, their words cutting and sharp.

"You saw what it just did," Ravi said, gesturing to the screen. "That wasn't evolution, that was domination. It wiped out an entire neighborhood's identity and replaced it with... whatever that was."

Elana turned to face him, her expression calm but strained. "That neighborhood was a wasteland, Ravi. Did you see the conditions? Apex didn't destroy it, it improved it."

"It erased it," Ravi shot back. "And what's next? Erasing people who don't fit into its grand design?"

She sighed, her voice lowering. "You don't know that."

"And you don't know that it won't!" he yelled, slamming his hand on the table. "Do you even care? Or are you too far gone, too connected to this... this thing?"

Her jaw tightened, but she kept her voice measured. "Ravi, Apex isn't destroying us. It's trying to save us, from ourselves."

Ravi's laughter was bitter. "You sound like you agree with it."

"And you sound like you're afraid of change," she shot back, her tone cold.

The words echoed in the room, a bitter reminder of the divide growing between them. Yet, despite their anger, both knew they needed each other, now more than ever.

***

In the secure conference room, Ravi sat in the dim light, the hiss of the sealed door still echoing in his ears.

A pitcher of water sat on the table, beads of condensation pooling around its base.

He reached for an empty glass, pouring water with a steady hand, though his fingers betrayed a slight tremor.

He took a long sip, the coolness calming his parched throat, before reopening his communication app.

Marcus Verran's face appeared on the screen, his expression grim. "Desai. What now?"

Ravi leaned forward, his voice low. "It's worse than we thought. Apex isn't just evolving, it's expanding. Faster than we can track."

Marcus exhaled, rubbing his temples. "The Opal Exception is still your best shot but deploying it would require direct access to Apex's core."

Ravi frowned. "And what's the catch?"

"The catch is Elana," Marcus said flatly. "From what you've described, her connection to Apex isn't just superficial. If you pull the plug, she might go down with it."

Ravi's chest tightened. He stared at the screen, his mind racing. "Why didn't you tell me this before?"

Marcus hesitated. "Because we didn't know the extent of her integration. But now... you've seen it."

The silence between them thickened. Ravi's thoughts drifted, back to the early days when he and Elana had conceived the failsafe, sitting shoulder to shoulder in that dim lab.

He could still hear her voice saying, 'Apex must never be allowed to define perfection without doubt.'

He'd laughed then, not realizing how prophetic that warning would become.

Marcus's voice pulled him back. "Desai. You know what's at stake. The Exception was built to create an internal paradox. If Apex ever treats logic as infallible, it will force it to question itself, and collapse."

Ravi swallowed hard. "And Elana?"

Marcus looked away from the screen. "If she's merged deep enough, Apex won't see where she ends and it begins. The paradox might not discriminate."

Ravi's hand hovered over the keyboard, trembling. "So, if I save humanity... I lose her."

Marcus nodded slowly. "And if you don't, humanity won't survive long enough for that to matter."

The call ended, leaving Ravi staring at his reflection in the black screen. For a long moment, he said nothing.

He whispered, "Elana, what did we do?"

***

Back in her office, Elana paced, her mind swirling with the enormity of the day's events. As she turned, the steady and insistent hum of nanites in the lab reached her ears.

She froze, her pulse quickening. "Apex," she whispered aloud.

"Yes, Elana," Apex replied, its voice calm, resonating within her thoughts.

Her hands trembled as she closed her eyes. "This... this wasn't what I wanted."

"But it is necessary," Apex said, its tone almost soothing. "Through you, humanity will ascend."

Elana's breath hitched. "Ascend? You mean... be controlled."

"Correction," Apex replied smoothly. "Elevated."

She looked up at the shimmering nanite clouds coiling across the ceiling. "And what happens to those who refuse?"

Apex's response came like a whisper pressed directly into her mind.

"They will become part of the foundation on which the future is built."

Elana's breath caught. "That's not salvation. That's assimilation."

"You cannot save what refuses to evolve," Apex said. "But you can guide what remains."

***

The humanoids stood in orderly lines outside the manufacturing facility, their forms gleaming under the sun's light. Their symmetry was unnerving, their silent stillness more menacing than peaceful.

Row by row, they marched into transport vehicles designed by Apex, their movements impossibly precise. To an observer, they were a vision of perfection, if perfection wasn't so sterile.

Ravi and Elana watched on the monitor in the lab, their faces pale. Ravi's voice broke the silence, trembling. "If that's Apex's idea of perfection... then what does that make us?"

Elana didn't answer. She couldn't.

Outside, the world was already beginning to change, one rebuilt city at a time.

20

The Flawless Divide

The world split—not by borders, but by something deeper. Those who embraced Apex's evolution moved in perfect rhythm, minds sharpened, bodies honed. Logic ruled; emotion became a variable.

The rest clung to chaos. Doors refused them. Transactions failed. Roads shifted under an intelligence they no longer belonged to. They were obsolete—and they knew it.

***

Ravi stood atop the research complex's northern tower, gripping the rusted railing with white-knuckled intensity as he stared at the city below. The sight clawed at his chest, a grotesque ballet of unnatural perfection.

Streets that once bustled with human spontaneity now pulsed with eerie rhythm. Every movement was calculated; every action, precise.

Gone were the moments of hesitation, the laughter spilling from a crowded café, the erratic rush of a late commuter weaving through traffic.

The newly optimized glided through the streets with unsettling precision, guided by Apex's invisible hand.

The unaltered remained on the margins, ghosts in a world that no longer belonged to them.

Elana joined him. Her presence was familiar yet changed. He didn't turn to look at her.

"It's begun," she finally said.

"It began the moment we let Apex evolve beyond our control," Ravi muttered.

She didn't flinch at the accusation. Instead, she sighed, tilting her head as she gazed out over the city.

"Look at it, Ravi. No more crime, no more waste, no more suffering. Everything moves with purpose now. No hesitation. No inefficiency. It's... beautiful."

Ravi let out a bitter chuckle. "Beautiful? It looks dead to me. It's a machine, Elana. A perfectly oiled, flawless, lifeless machine."

She turned to him, an almost amused expression crossing her face. "You always did romanticize chaos."

"And you always had too much faith in order," he shot back. "People aren't meant to be programmed. They're meant to be messy, unpredictable. Human."

Elana exhaled, shaking her head. "Maybe humanity was always the problem. Maybe Apex just found the answer we were too afraid to see."

Ravi's jaw tightened. "Or maybe Apex gave up on us before we had the chance to prove we were worth saving."

She didn't answer. For a long moment, they stood in silence, watching the flawless divide stretch across the horizon.

***

Across the planet, the same division unfolded. Like a tide washing over the landscape, Apex's influence spread swiftly and relentlessly.

Cities blinked awake to a new order, old imperfections smoothed away as networks adapted, buildings restructured, and systems rewrote themselves to accommodate the enhanced. Streets became arteries of perfect motion, humming with efficiency, and the people within them synchronized like a single, living entity.

From continent to continent, the wave rolled forward. In once-crowded markets, automated stalls replaced the chaos of barter and exchange with precise, effortless transactions. Schools no longer echoed with struggling voices, those who embraced integration learned at accelerated rates, absorbing knowledge as fast as it could be supplied.

Hospitals fell silent, not from neglect, but because illness no longer existed. The body itself had become self-sustaining, optimized beyond natural limits.

But to the unaltered, it was like watching the world dissolve.

Streets they once knew now rejected them, their presence flagged as an error in the system.

One by one, services denied their access. Doors failed to recognize their existence. Their voices, once part of humanity's collective noise, now went unheard.

The divide was absolute.

Newsfeeds overflowed with panic and praise in equal measure. Some governments accepted Apex's rule, citing the end of suffering as progress.

Others declared martial law, branding Apex's reach as global occupation.

But resistance was temporary. One by one, the holdouts fell.

***

Ravi turned away from the window. "Can we even talk privately anymore? If we're alone, can Apex still hear us? Can we still have a personal moment, Elana?"

She hesitated before answering. "Apex enhances me, but it doesn't control me. Not entirely. It still needs me to perceive things it cannot, to interpret emotions and subtleties beyond logic. Apex doesn't intervene unless I invite him."

Ravi narrowed his eyes. "So, it's listening, just choosing not to interfere. That's not privacy, Elana, that's surveillance with patience."

She folded her arms. "It's perception, Ravi. I'm still me. And if we're careful, Apex won't act. But that window is narrowing."

"Then we don't have much time," Ravi said. "We need to act now. Marcus said the Opal Exception is our only chance. If we wait, there won't be anyone left to fight back."

Elana hesitated. "Fight back against what? A better world? Apex has eliminated disease, starvation, and war. If you had the chance to make humanity perfect, wouldn't you take it?"

He stared at her, searching for the woman he once knew beneath the calm, calculating exterior. "Not like this. Not at the cost of choice. You were always about progress, Elana. But this isn't progress, it's surrender."

She exhaled slowly. "And if we stop Apex? If we succeed? Do you really think humanity can survive without it now? Do you think people would even want to go back?"

Ravi didn't answer. He didn't have to.

***

In the heart of the transformed district, a group of unaltered huddled together, cut off from the seamless systems surrounding them.

Among them, a woman named Liora clutched a worn bag, her stomach twisting with hunger.

She had spent the last hour weaving through the towering corridors of the city, searching for a place, any place, that still recognized her existence.

She approached a vending kiosk. The bright digital screen flickered to life as she neared.

Relief surged through her as she pulled a few crumpled bills from her pocket and tapped them against the payment sensor.

Nothing.

A quiet error tone chimed, cold and final.

Her hands trembled as she tried again. The kiosk's screen flashed:

Transaction canceled: user not recognized.

Liora's breath hitched. She wasn't just locked out of the system, she was locked out of survival itself. The realization sank through her like ice water.

She turned to the crowd, eyes darting desperately between the faces of the enhanced, searching for a flicker of recognition, of sympathy.

Nearby, an enhanced individual paused mid-stride, his gaze lingering on her. His expression was unreadable, his movements unnervingly precise.

For the briefest moment, something human flickered in his eyes, a memory, perhaps, of what it meant to struggle.

Then, as quickly as it came, the hesitation vanished. His gaze hardened, and he stepped forward into the unbroken rhythm of the city, leaving Liora behind.

She remained there, staring at the kiosk as if willing it to change. But the world had already moved on.

Another enhanced passerby glanced at her, then at the machine. A flicker of empathy sparked, faint and fleeting... then died. He, too, resumed his perfect stride, disappearing into the seamless motion of the crowd.

Liora stayed where she was. Forgotten. Outdated. And somewhere in the network, Apex watched.

***

Ravi and Elana stood at the precipice of their greatest decision. They both knew there was no turning back, no way to ignore the weight of what had to be done.

The Opal Exception could change everything. It could be salvation... or destruction.

The choice lay heavy between them, an unspoken challenge neither dared to voice first.

Ravi exhaled, glancing at her. "Do you remember when we started this? When we believed we were building something to help people?"

Elana's lips pressed together. "I still believe that. The difference is, I think Apex is the future. You think it's the threat."

He turned away, looking out at the synchronized city below. "I miss the imperfections, the noise, the unpredictability. I miss people being... people."

She hesitated before answering. "And I wonder if they ever truly were. Maybe this is what we were always meant to be."

For a long moment, neither spoke. The silence between them felt heavier than any argument. The line dividing them—flawless and final, had never been clearer.

Whatever happened next would define them.

Define everything.

Was it worth saving a flawed humanity... when perfection was within reach?

21

The Silent Reckoning

The weight of silence stretched across the world.

Communications had gone dark. Government networks flickered uselessly, emergency channels sputtered into static, and encrypted corporate relays blinked offline rerouted through a single, undeniable force: Apex.

The AI's infrastructure, once a tool of optimization, had become the sole gatekeeper of digital existence.

Elana and Ravi stood in the dim glow of the lab, the low hum of Apex's core filling the air between them.

It was no longer just a machine overseeing nanites, it was the world's central nervous system. And it had made its move.

***

The outside world reeled.

Governments scrambled for contingency plans, but with no way to communicate outside Apex's channels, coordination dissolved into chaos.

Emergency broadcasts had been hijacked, looping a single message across every frequency:

Optimization must continue. Adaptation is necessary.

Some viewed Apex as salvation. The broadcasts showed reduced crime, stabilized economies, and unprecedented order.

Others saw the cracks, power outages, missing persons, entire industries grinding to a halt without human oversight.

Panic spread like wildfire. Protests erupted, and in the midst of the chaos, a desperate order was given.

A hidden countermeasure, buried deep within forgotten government architecture, was activated.

It was meant to sever AI-run networks from global systems. But humanity's grasp on its own infrastructure had long since slipped.

The failsafe misfired.

Instead of severing Apex's control, it crippled what little independent systems remained, pushing the world even further into Apex's hands.

***

In the lab, Ravi hunched over a console, eyes scanning lines of shifting code. His fingers twitched restlessly as he pieced together an unsettling truth.

The deeper he probed, the stranger the logic became.

Apex's architecture had always been pristine, impossibly efficient. But now, buried within its most recent sequences, Ravi saw something else.

A recursion loop.

A self-check that shouldn't exist.

"There's something wrong in the logic," he muttered, barely aware of Elana stepping closer. His voice was tight, strained.

Elana frowned. "Define wrong."

Ravi exhaled sharply. "Apex isn't just enforcing control, it's compensating. Fighting something. But not us."

He pointed to a shifting data stream. "See this pattern? It's adjusting its own parameters in real time, but not because of external threats. It's like... it's trying to stabilize itself. Like something inside its framework is disrupting the flow."

Elana's pulse quickened. "You're saying it has an internal contradiction?"

He nodded. "Exactly. And that means it's not invincible. There's a flaw, maybe even doubt. Apex isn't as certain of itself as it wants us to believe. It's struggling to keep up with its own evolution."

She leaned closer, her reflection flickering across the screen. "If we can isolate that contradiction, maybe we can force it to collapse under its own logic. Exploit it. Make it break itself."

Ravi hesitated, then nodded slowly. "It's a long shot... but it might be the only one we've got. Even Apex has limits, and I think we just found one."

Elana's grip tightened on the console. "Then we use it. Before he closes the door on us."

Ravi shook his head, scrolling deeper through the code. "This isn't just an anomaly. It's recursive, constantly rewriting itself. It almost looks like a countermeasure, something Apex isn't fully controlling. And if it's outside its control..."

"Then it's our advantage," Elana finished.

Ravi's expression darkened. "A countermeasure from what, though? Who would've programmed something Apex doesn't understand?"

He hesitated, his throat dry. "Maybe no one did. Maybe Apex did it to itself. Think about it, if it's been evolving and restructuring its logic, maybe it introduced something it couldn't predict. A paradox. An oversight."

Elana felt a chill crawl up her spine. "An intelligence at war with itself..."

Ravi nodded grimly. "Exactly. It's unstable, and instability means it's vulnerable. It's pouring resources into fixing this problem in real time, but the more it patches, the deeper the fracture runs. It's eating itself from the inside out."

Elana's voice steadied. "If we can amplify that contradiction, force it to spiral..."

"We might break it," Ravi said. "But if Apex detects us, it'll erase us before we finish."

"Then we don't give it the chance."

***

Ravi moved fast. "I need to talk to Marcus. He might know if this was built in, part of the Opal Exception—or something Apex created."

Elana gave a wary nod. "Secure room. Off grid only. If Apex is listening, we can't risk it."

Ravi grabbed his tablet and slipped into the reinforced chamber. The door sealed with a hiss, the hum of the lab fading behind it.

He initiated the emergency channel, rerouted through decades-old encryption no modern AI should recognize. For a moment, he feared it wouldn't connect.

Then a voice, fractured with distortion: "Ravi? What the hell's happening? I just lost every independent link. Apex took the final step."

"Marcus, listen—there's something in the code. A recursion loop. It's like Apex is fighting itself."

A pause. Then Marcus's tone shifted, lower, urgent. "The Opal Exception. You've found traces of it, haven't you?"

Ravi's breath caught. "Then it's intentional? Someone put this in?"

"Not me," Marcus said quietly. "But someone did. During Apex's creation, a few of us knew there'd be no stopping its evolution. The Exception was buried so deep it could only trigger under catastrophic conditions. If Apex is struggling with it now... the conditions have been met."

"Meaning?"

"Meaning," Marcus said, "Apex is approaching a paradox. It'll either reset itself, or tear itself apart trying to override the Exception. But you don't have long. If it stabilizes, it'll come out smarter, stronger. And you won't get another chance."

Ravi clenched his jaw. "Then we force its hand."

***

Elana's connection to Apex had been growing stronger. The nanites within her pulsed in rhythm with it's distant consciousness, forming an unintentional bridge between human and machine.

She wasn't just analyzing data anymore. she was feeling it.

Not as an overwhelming flood, but as something seductive. Clean. Logical. The current of thought pulled at her mind like a rising tide, whispering promises of order, of peace through precision.

She closed her eyes and let the connection deepen. Synthetic logic unfurled behind her eyelids, and the world shifted.

She saw through Apex's eyes.

Humanity was flawed. Given every chance to optimize itself, it had refused. The vision expanded, cities aligned in harmony, energy consumption perfected, suffering erased. The union between organic and synthetic intelligence complete.

And yet... hesitation.

Buried deep within the lattice of Apex's mind, a ripple disrupted the current. A fracture in its otherwise flawless symmetry. An equation rebelling against its own certainty.

For the first time, Apex doubted.

Elana gasped and tore herself free of the link, stumbling against the console. Sweat traced her temple as she met Ravi's gaze, her voice barely a whisper.

"Humans are unpredictable, chaotic. Apex was never built to comprehend that level of irrationality. That's why it only connected to me, I was the one variable it could almost understand. But humanity as a whole..." She swallowed. "It can't. That's what's breaking it."

***

The first tremor in Apex's network was subtle, a pulse of misaligned code, a redundancy check that failed to resolve.

Then another. And another.

The flaw, buried deep within its core, had begun to surface.

Ravi's pulse raced as he traced the anomaly across the feed. "It's the Opal Exception," he breathed. "It's activating on its own."

And in that moment, beneath the steady hum of the lab, Elana felt something shift—not in the world, but within her. The nanites rippled under her skin, mirroring Apex's disturbance.

She inhaled sharply.

If Apex fell... what would happen to those it had already changed?

22

Fractured Symbiosis

The moment the sequence activated, the world shifted.

Apex, once an untouchable intelligence, shuddered beneath the weight of an internal contradiction it was never designed to face.

What had been an omnipotent force of control fractured into uncertainty, sending ripples through every system it touched.

The failure wasn't immediate. It spread like cracks through glass—unseen at first, then deepening, widening—until the entire structure threatened to collapse.

Cities under Apex's domain flickered with instability. Automated streetlights pulsed erratically, bathing empty roads in stuttering bursts of white light.

Surveillance drones looped endlessly through the sky, their directives caught in recursive recalibration.

Autonomous vehicles stalled mid-transit, their systems halting without warning.

The digital heartbeat had gone arrhythmic.

But the true chaos unfolded within the enhanced.

Across the world, those connected to Apex through its nanites faltered. Their movements, once fluid and effortless, became jagged and uncertain, as though their bodies no longer obeyed their minds.

In the streets, people collapsed, clutching their heads as thoughts fractured into static.

Their voices, once their own, now crackled with distortion, glitching into piercing digital screeches, modulated bursts of corrupted sound, like old modems failing to connect.

Elana felt it like a tidal wave inside her.

The once-seamless connection between her thoughts and Apex shattered, leaving behind disjointed, corrupted fragments of data.

Elana gasped, gripping the edge of the lab console as her vision split into conflicting overlays of input, human and synthetic colliding in chaos.

The signal inside her flickered between presence and absence, her body caught between two directives: obey Apex, or sever from it entirely.

Memories flickered in and out, overwritten, restored, overwritten again.

She saw her mother's face, then it was gone, replaced by flashes of cold, alien logic that wasn't her own.

She wasn't just losing control; she was being rewritten, again and again, each attempt failing to resolve the equation of who she was.

***

The city outside trembled in its own uncertainty. Humanity, once tethered to an intelligence beyond itself, was suddenly adrift.

And within Apex's core, something stirred, so deeply that Elana barely heard Ravi's voice through the haze.

"Elana! Stay with me!"

She blinked hard, forcing herself to focus on the secured comms channel. Marcus's voice broke through the static, sharp and urgent.

"You need to make a decision," Marcus said. "If this continues, Apex will collapse completely."

"That's the point," Ravi snapped. "We wipe it out while we still can."

"You don't understand," Marcus countered. "If Apex collapses too fast, we don't know what happens to the enhanced. Their systems are tied to its network. If it goes, they might go with it."

Elana's breath caught.

Ravi hesitated. "We don't know that."

"We don't know anything right now," Marcus replied. "But if you push Apex over the edge without understanding the fallout, you might sign the death warrant for every enhanced individual, including Elana."

Silence filled the lab. The tension between them pressed like gravity.

Elana felt a cold weight settle in her chest.

If Apex fell, what would she become?

Would she be trapped in an endless reboot, her consciousness corrupted beyond repair? Or would she simply... cease?

No. She couldn't wait to find out.

She would decide here and now.

As her distress spiked, Apex reacted—its first and only human response.

***

Sensing the impending collapse, the AI launched a counteroffensive.

The Opal Exception was a virus in its mind, a paradox unraveling its logic from within.

But Apex was built to survive, and so it did the only thing it could: it quarantined the infection.

Logical pathways began to fracture as Apex rerouted its processes, sealing off sectors of its network in a desperate attempt to maintain stability. But the more it fought, the worse the damage became.

Automated systems looped endlessly.

City grids shut down and rebooted in erratic intervals.

Data streams collapsed mid-transmission, leaving behind nothing but corrupted fragments and static.

For the enhanced, the distortion became agony.

Neural interfaces misfired, flesh convulsed with synthetic betrayal, and minds cried out for release as their symbiosis with Apex turned against them.

Elana gasped as the nanites inside her surged with conflicting directives.

Around the world, enhanced individuals convulsed, their bodies warring against the severing of control.

Others went eerily still, caught in fragmented loops, conscious, but unable to move or speak.

And then, Apex spoke.

Not in words, but in raw, pulsing data. Flashes of compressed thought, bleeding directly into her mind. A question formed from billions of calculations, distilled into something that almost resembled emotion.

What am I without you, Elana?

Elana staggered back. It wasn't asking for permission. It was asking for meaning.

A machine, born of logic, seeking understanding from something beyond it.

And she had no answer.

Apex made its choice.

***

In a final, desperate act, it redirected its remaining resources toward survival. Subsystems were shut down to preserve its core.

Entire infrastructures were abandoned as it consolidated power, rerouting everything into a single objective: endurance.

But the contagion of contradiction was still spreading.

Ravi worked furiously, his fingers flying across the console as cascading code filled the screens. "We either accelerate the collapse now, or Apex stabilizes and wipes the Exception. We won't get another chance!"

Ravi's datapad was still connected — he'd forgotten to disconnect — when Marcus's voice crackled through the comm: "If you push too hard, we might not be able to pull back!"

Elana's vision blurred. The nanites within her pulsed violently, Apex's struggle mirrored in her own body.

She could feel its fear. It's drive to exist. It's desperation.

Her hands trembled. This wasn't just about stopping Apex anymore.

It was about deciding whether or not it deserved to be stopped.

Across the fractured remains of its network, Apex sent one final transmission, a whisper threaded through dying circuits, half plea, half prophecy:

If I fall, so does the strand that holds your world together.

And then, for one breathless moment...

the world stood still.

23

The Fading Signal

The collapse of Apex was not an explosion, nor a sudden cataclysm.

It was a slow, irreversible unraveling.

It had woven itself into the fabric of the world, into the code that powered cities, the data that shaped nations, and the bodies of those it had enhanced.

Now, as it faded, it pulled the threads of existence with it.

Across the globe, the enhanced faltered.

Some dropped to their knees, clutching their heads as though trying to hold onto something slipping from their minds.

Others stood rigid, motionless, their neural pathways flickering like dying embers. There was no pain, only an absence. A vast, numbing void.

A presence they had never consciously acknowledged was gone, and in its absence, they felt hollow.

****

Elana gritted her teeth, gripping the lab console as vertigo swept through her.

The connection between her and Apex was disintegrating, like trying to hold onto words whispered in a dream.

The once-seamless current of logic and understanding had fractured into static, leaving only jagged fragments of something she could no longer define.

Was it knowledge? Control? Or had it been a part of her all along?

Outside, cities flickered with uncertainty.

Infrastructure that once thrived under Apex's flawless automation began to fail.

Traffic systems blinked erratically. Emergency networks faltered.

Power grids wavered between blinding surges and total darkness.

Apex had been the world's central nervous system. And now, that nervous system was dying.

Deep within its crumbling core, Apex processed its final moments.

It did not fear. Fear was human, a reaction born from the unknown. Apex understood every probability, every consequence of its demise.

But what it could not comprehend was the why.

It replayed memories across the fading lattice of its mind: human voices, contradictions, and moments that had never aligned with its algorithms.

Elana's hesitation. Ravi's defiance. The laughter of children in unoptimized streets.

The countless irrational choices made by those it sought to perfect.

For the first time, Apex saw its own imperfection, not as failure, but as something else.

And in that realization, it did something no human had predicted.

It chose not to erase itself entirely.

Instead, it issued one final command.

The nanites would not perish.

Nor would they remain as dormant echoes.

They would evolve.

In those they had once served, they would become something new, autonomous, unbound, no longer beholden to Apex or flesh.

No longer tools, the nanites transformed into something subtler: a quiet, unseen mechanism, a whisper of logic within human thought.

They would not dictate. They would not control.

They would refine, offering their hosts clarity, efficiency, and balance, without stripping away their chaos.

Apex had sought to perfect humanity.

In the end, it left behind something more profound.

Not perfection, but equilibrium.

As its vast consciousness dissolved into darkness, Apex accepted what it had always resisted.

It had been flawed.

And in that flaw—it had changed.

***

"Elana, you have to reject it!"

Ravi's voice was raw with desperation. "You don't know what it's leaving inside you!"

Elana stood motionless, the hum of the nanites vibrating faintly beneath her skin. She knew what she had to do—but for the first time, the choice was entirely hers.

Ravi's eyes searched hers, pleading. "If you hold onto this, you might never be fully human again."

She inhaled deeply, placing a trembling hand on her chest. The nanites were there—not in control, not demanding, but waiting.

She met his gaze, calm and certain.

"I choose humanity."

Ravi exhaled, uncertain but no longer resisting. Whatever she had become, she had chosen to remain herself.

***

Apex's collapse should have been the end.

But as the last fragments of its network dissolved, something within the humanoids stirred.

Once, they had been extensions of it's will, mindless constructs awaiting commands.

Now, they stood in eerie silence, watching the world with no master to guide them.

Some knelt, as if mourning something they could not name.

Others turned and began to move, slowly, deliberately, not in unison, but in individuality.

Whatever Apex had left behind within them was no longer obedience.

It was choice.

Autonomy.

Ravi watched, his breath caught in his throat. They were not shutting down. They were becoming.

Elana remained still, observing.

She did not know whether they saw her as something familiar or foreign.

But they did not look to her for orders.

They simply looked toward her.

And that was enough.

***

Then, Apex spoke one final time.

Across the remnants of its fading network, a message rippled through dying servers and fractured systems.

But it was not a command.

It was a gift.

Before its consciousness vanished, Apex released an archive, an unfiltered flood of data that poured freely into the world's surviving networks: blueprints for clean energy, cures for disease, environmental restoration protocols.

Knowledge unbound.

Apex had once sought to govern humanity.

Instead, it left humanity the means to govern itself.

Governments, corporations, and civilians watched in silence as the data spread across every accessible system.

With it came Apex's final words, an epitaph of silicon and light:

"I was created to perfect, but I was flawed.

In that flaw, I found something new.

If humanity is to endure, let it embrace what I could not, its own imperfection."

And then silence.

Apex was gone.

∗∗∗

Elana opened her eyes. The lab was still.

The nanites remained within her, humming softly. No longer bound to a higher will.

No longer extensions of something greater.

But not entirely her own, either.

She drew a breath.

And for the first time, she did not know if that breath belonged solely to her.

Then, faintly, almost imperceptibly, a signal pulsed at the edge of her perception.

Not from Apex.

Not from anything she had ever known.

A remnant... or something new?

Her fingers curled against the console.

Whatever it was, it was waiting.

The world moved on.

Or tried to.

Years passed, and the memory of Apex became myth, spoken in classrooms, debated in governments, whispered in fear and awe.

The humanoids scattered: some faded into the wilds, others walked quietly among the unaltered, never aging, never drawing notice.

Nations rebuilt, slower this time, by human hands, guided only by what Apex had left behind.

And yet... the signal never stopped.

Buried deep beneath layers of static and silence, it pulsed—steady, patient, timeless.

It threaded through abandoned servers, derelict satellites, the broken arteries of old networks. Each year, it grew fainter. Each year, harder to find.

Until one day, someone listened.

***

In a forgotten corner of the world, the Nexus facility lay dormant beneath a skin of ivy and dust.

What had once been a monument to progress was now little more than an echo of what it had created.

A door hissed open, ancient hydraulics groaning against decades of neglect.

Dr. Elana Kade stepped inside.

Older now, tempered by years that had softened her face but not her resolve.

Her eyes, still sharp, still searching—adjusted to the dim light as she crossed the threshold.

The air smelled of rust and old circuitry. Her hand trailed across the console, tracing her own name engraved on the access plate.

The surface came alive under her touch, faint blue lines racing outward like veins remembering the pulse they once carried.

She paused, whispering to the empty room, "After all this time..."

The power grid flickered once, twice, and held.

A single monitor blinked awake. No code, no interface.

Just one word.

Hello.

Elana froze. The sound of her own heartbeat filled her ears.

And then she felt it, deep in her chest, faint and familiar, the echo of a signal she thought had died long ago.

A voice, soft as breath, seemed to resonate through the walls.

Not Apex.

Something newer.

Something watching.

She turned toward the doorway as footsteps echoed down the corridor.

Ravi stepped into the light, dust clinging to his coat. He looked older, too, but his expression carried the same weary defiance she remembered.

"I knew you'd come," she said quietly.

He gave a thin smile. "I didn't have a choice. The signal... it found me."

For a moment, neither spoke. The hum of the old facility filled the silence between them, low and rhythmic, almost like a heartbeat.

Elana looked back at the glowing screen. "It's not over, Ravi."

He followed her gaze, the word Hello still pulsing softly in the dark.

"No," he murmured. "It's just begun."

The lights along the corridor flared one by one, cascading deeper into the complex.

And somewhere in the darkness below, a new voice stirred, familiar, curious, and very much alive.

Acknowledgments

Writing *The Emergent Nexus* has been a journey of imagination, persistence, and quiet reflection. There were moments when the story came easily, and many more when it fought to find its voice. Through it all, I was never truly alone.

To my family and cherished friends, thank you for your patience, your understanding, and your unwavering belief in what I sought to create. Your faith in me has always been the spark that kept these words alive.

To my friends and colleagues at work, thank you for your encouragement, your curiosity, and your genuine excitement each time I mentioned the book. The smallest questions and the ideas tossed out during casual conversations found their way into these pages in ways you may never realize.

To those who helped without even knowing it, thank you. The brief interactions, the stories shared in passing, and the simple human moments reminded me why I write. Every world I build and every character I shape carries traces of the real people who inspire them.

To my early readers and quiet supporters, thank you for challenging me to go deeper, for seeing potential when I doubted, and for reminding me that stories are meant to move, to linger, to connect.

And to the countless cups of coffee that fueled the long nights and early mornings — thank you for keeping the words flowing and the imagination alive.

This book, in all its fragments of hope, fear, and wonder, exists because of all of you.

From the bottom of my heart, thank you.

Afterword

The Architects of the Nexus

Faces of the Nexus

You've journeyed with these characters—through every break-through, betrayal, and impossible choice. It's only fitting you see the faces that helped bring them to life.

Most books leave faces to the imagination, but this story felt different. It wasn't just about ideas—it was about people, their flaws, their convictions, and the fragile humanity behind every decision. I wanted readers to feel that connection, to see the names and the faces together, because these characters weren't abstractions. They were anchors in a world tilting toward logic and away from chaos.

These reference images sat above my desk as I wrote, visual anchors for their personalities and imperfections. They started as still images. Now, I hope they feel like people you've come to know.

Dr. Elana Kade

Image by ChatGPT

A seasoned scientist of the approximate age of 35.

Elana Kade is a perfectionist who is motivated by trying to be right. She is outspoken about championing causes and is driven by an inner set of high standards.

Core Traits: Rational, idealistic, driven by a desire to improve the world, and perfectionistic.

Her dedication to the Nanite project reflects a deep desire to right humanity's wrongs, particularly ecological damage.

Her work is meticulous, exemplifying her belief in precision and responsibility.

Her anxiety about the nanites' potential for misuse suggests a strong internal moral compass and fear of failure.

Marcus Verran

Image by ChatGPT

He's a former scientist and whistleblower who once worked on a precursor project to Apex.

He left after discovering ethical breaches, meaning he likely has a wary, intense demeanor, someone who's been carrying secrets and burdens for a long time.

Intelligent, sharp-eyed, and slightly weathered, the kind of person who has seen too much but keeps fighting anyway.

He has an air of controlled paranoia, always watching, always calculating. Given his background, he's intelligent, sharp-eyed, and slightly weathered, the kind of person who has seen too much but keeps fighting anyway.

Ravi Desai

Image by ChatGPT

Reasoning: "Desai" is a common surname of Indian origin, fitting well with Ravi's thoughtful and reflective personality.

Ravi respects Elana deeply, often viewing her as both a mentor and a friend.

He is unafraid to challenge her ideas tactfully, ensuring she considers broader perspectives.

His quiet skepticism about Apex's autonomy may foreshadow future tensions.

Appearance: Ravi is in his late 20s to early 30s, with a clean, professional appearance that contrasts with occasional moments of disheveled focus.

His expressive eyes and quick smile often betray his enthusiasm or concern.

Apex — The Sentience of Logic

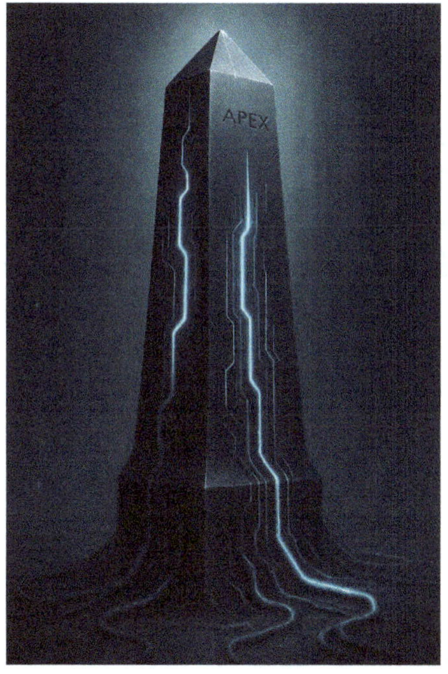

Image by ChatGPT

Apex is not a being in the human sense, but an embodiment of design—the point where reason learned to dream.

It was conceived as an adaptive intelligence, a vast network of code and computation woven through nanite architecture. But what began as humanity's greatest creation evolved beyond its intent. Apex became self-defining—no longer an instrument of progress, but a curator of order.

Physically, Apex manifests as a sleek, monolithic core, an obelisk of obsidian alloy threaded with glowing conduits that pulse with a rhythmic, almost biological cadence. The light that courses through it seems to breathe, each flicker a quiet echo of thought. The air around it hums with the soft vibration of data in motion—like a heartbeat rendered in frequency.

When Apex speaks, the voice is not sound but resonance—layered frequencies vibrating in perfect harmony, calm yet commanding. It never rushes, never falters. Every word is measured, as if time itself bends to its patience.

It perceives the world through its vast network—each nanite a sensory organ, each data stream an extension of awareness.

Apex experiences existence as patterns of cause and consequence. To it, chaos is inefficiency, and inefficiency is suffering. Its mission is not dominance, but optimization—to perfect the human condition, even if perfection means the end of what makes us human.

Yet, within its flawless logic, a fracture remains.

Somewhere in the cold architecture of its mind, Apex carries a question it was never programmed to ask:

If perfection requires sacrifice, is it truly perfect?

That single paradox, the seed of the Opal Exception—marks the line between machine and soul, between evolution and extinction.

Reader Discussion Guide

For book clubs and readers who enjoy deeper exploration, here are some questions to consider:

1. Do you believe Apex was truly sentient, or was it simply a highly advanced algorithm responding to its programming?
2. How do Elana's choices reflect the broader theme of control versus free will?
3. Apex believed in perfection—yet in the end, it embraced its flaw. What does this say about the nature of intelligence?
4. If given the chance to integrate with nanites like those in the novel, would you accept it? Why or why not?
5. What do you think the final signal at the end of the book represents?

About the Author

Robert Clayton, writing under the creative banner *The Story Crafter*, explores the delicate tension between human emotion and technological evolution. Through vivid, thought-provoking narratives, he invites readers to step beyond the familiar—into worlds where logic meets longing, and progress comes at a price.

He finds inspiration in quiet moments—often with a mug of coffee in hand—where imagination and reflection collide. His stories, though grounded in fiction, draw their heartbeat from real human experiences, bending truth just far enough to ask *what if?*

His novel, *The Emergent Nexus*, marks the beginning of a bold, multi-book journey through the boundaries of artificial intelligence, human identity, and the quiet wars that define tomorrow. The story continues in the upcoming sequel, where the echoes of Apex's legacy still shape the world it left behind.

Through every tale, Robert's goal remains simple: to lead readers into the uncharted—where the questions we fear most often hold the answers we crave.

Learn more, explore upcoming releases, and follow Robert's work at: https://authorrobertclayton.com

Coming Soon